Out of
Sight,

Out of
Time

ALSO BY ALLY CARTER

The Gallagher Girls series:

I'd Tell You I Love You, But Then I'd Have to Kill You

Cross My Heart and Hope to Spy

Don't Judge a Girl by Her Cover

Only the Good Spy Young

The Heist Society series:

Heist Society

Uncommon Criminals

Perfect Scoundrels

Out of Sight, Out of Time

ally carter

SCHOLASTIC INC.

ISBN 978-0-545-57125-8

12 11 10 9 8 7 6 5 4   14 15 16 17 18/0

Printed in the U.S.A.   40

This edition first printing, March 2013

This book is set in Goudy.

For Jen

Chapter One

"Where am I?"

I heard the words, but I wasn't sure I'd said them. The voice was too rough, too coarse to be mine. It was as if there were a stranger in my skin, lying in the dark, saying, "Who's there?"

"So it's English, is it?"

As soon as the young woman moved to stand at the end of the bed, I could see that she was beautiful. She had an Irish accent and strawberry blond hair in a shade that could never be anything but natural. Soft curls framed a slightly freckled face with blue eyes and a wide smile. Maybe it was the terrible throbbing in my head—the piercing pain behind my eyes—but I could have sworn I saw a halo.

"And American too, by the sound of it. Oh, Sister Isabella is going to be very upset about this. She wagered a week's worth of kitchen duty you were Australian. But you're not, are you?"

I shook my head, and it felt like a bomb went off. I wanted to scream, but instead I gritted my teeth and said, "You were betting on me?"

"Well, you should have heard yourself, talking in all kinds of tongues—like the devil himself was after you. French and German, Russian and Japanese, I think. A lot of languages no one here even speaks." She walked to the small wooden stool beside my bed and whispered, "You'll have to forgive us, but it was either bet . . . or worry."

There were soft sheets beneath my hands, a cold stone wall beside my right shoulder. A candle flickered in the corner, pale light washing partway across a sparsely furnished room, leaving it mostly in shadow.

Worry seemed appropriate under the circumstances.

"Who are you?" I asked, scooting backward on the thin mattress, retreating into the cold corner made of stone. I was too weak to fight, far too unsteady to run, but when the girl reached for me, I managed to grab her hand and twist her arm into a terrible angle. "What is this place?"

"It's my home." Her voice cracked, but she didn't try to fight. She just leaned closer to me, brought her free hand to my face, and said, *"You're okay."*

But I didn't feel okay. My head ached, and when I moved, pain shot down my side. I kicked off the covers and saw that my legs were a solid mass of bruises and gashes and scrapes. Someone had bandaged my right ankle, packed it in ice. Someone had cleaned my cuts. Someone had brought me to that bed and listened, guessing where I had come from and why.

Someone was looking right at me. "You did this?"

I ran my hand down my leg, fingering the gauze that bound my ankle.

"I did." The girl placed a hand over my fingers as they picked at the threads. "Don't you go undoing it, now."

A crucifix hung on the wall behind her, and when she smiled, it was perhaps the kindest look I'd ever seen.

"You're a nun?" I asked.

"I will be soon. I hope." She blushed, and I realized she wasn't much older than I was. "By year's end, I should take my vows. I'm Mary, by the way."

"Is this a hospital, Mary?"

"Oh, no. But there isn't much in these parts, I'm afraid. So we do what we can."

"Who is *we*?"

A kind of terror seized me then. I pulled my knees close to my chest. My legs felt skinnier than they should have, my hands rougher than I remembered. Just a few days before, I'd let my roommates give me a manicure to take their minds off of finals week. Liz had chosen the color—Flamingo Pink—but when I looked at my fingers then, the polish was gone. Blood and dirt were caked under the nails as if I'd crawled out of my school and halfway across the world on my hands and knees to reach that narrow bed.

"How long..." My voice caught, so I tried again. "How long have I been here?"

"Now, now." Mary straightened the covers. She seemed afraid to face me when she said, "You don't need to worry about—"

"How long?" I shouted, and Mary dropped her voice and her gaze. Her hands were, at last, still.

"You've been here six days."

Six days, I thought. Not even a week. And yet it sounded like forever.

"Where are my clothes?" I pushed aside the covers and swung my feet to the floor, but my head felt so strange, I knew better than to try to stand. "I need my clothes and my things. I need . . ."

I wanted to explain, but the words failed me. *Thought* failed me. Once I got back to school, I was pretty sure my teachers would fail me. My head swirled, but I couldn't hear a thing over the sound of the music that filled the little room, pulsing too loudly inside my ears.

"Can you turn that down, please?"

"What?" the girl asked.

I closed my eyes and tried not to think about the melody I didn't know how to sing.

"Make it stop. Can you please make it stop?"

"Make what stop?"

"That music. It's so loud."

"Gillian"—the girl slowly shook her head—"there is no music."

I wanted to argue, but I couldn't. I wanted to run, but I had no clue to where. All I seemed able to do was sit quietly as Mary picked up my feet and gently placed them back on the bed.

"You've got quite a bump there. I'm not surprised you're hearing things. You've been saying things, too, just so you know. But I wouldn't worry about that. People hear and say all kinds of crazy things when they're sick."

"What did I say?" I asked, honestly terrified of the answer.

"It doesn't matter now." She tucked the covers in around me, just like Grandma Morgan used to do. "All you need to do is lie there and rest and—"

"What did I say?"

"Crazy things." The girl's voice was a whisper. "A lot of it we didn't understand. The rest—between us all—we pieced together."

"Like what?" I gripped her hand tightly, as if trying to squeeze the truth out.

"Like you go to a school for spies."

The woman who came to me next had swollen, arthritic fingers and gray eyes. She was followed by a young nun with red hair and a Hungarian accent, and a pair of twins in their late forties who huddled together and spoke Russian, low and under their breaths.

At my school, they call me the Chameleon. I'm the girl nobody sees. But not then. Not there. The sisters who surrounded me saw *everything*. They took my pulse and shined a bright light into my eyes. Someone brought a glass of water and instructed me to sip it very slowly. It was the sweetest stuff I'd ever tasted, and so I downed it all in one long gulp, but then I started choking—my head kept on throbbing—and the nun with the swollen fingers looked at me as if to say, *Told you so*.

I don't know whether it was the habits or the accents or the stern order that I should lie perfectly still, but I couldn't shake the feeling that I'd found myself surrounded by another ancient and powerful sisterhood. I knew better than to go against them, so I stayed where I was and did exactly as I was told.

After a long time, the girl who had been there at the beginning eased toward me and took a seat at the foot of my bed. "Do you know why you're here?"

Where's here? I wanted to say, but something in my spy blood told me not to.

"I was doing a sort of project for school. I had to split off from the others. I must have . . . lost my way." I felt my voice break and told myself it was okay. Even the Mother Superior couldn't blame me. Technically, it wasn't a lie.

"We're a bit worried about that head of yours," Mary said. "You may need surgery, tests, things we can't do here. And someone must be looking for you."

I thought about my mother and my friends, and finally, about the Circle of Cavan. I looked down at my broken body and wondered if maybe I'd already been found. Then I studied the innocent faces that surrounded me and felt a whole new surge of panic: *What if the Circle finds me here?*

"Gillian?" Mary said. It was an embarrassingly long time before I realized she was speaking to me. "Gillian, are you okay?"

But I was already moving, pushing off the bed and across the room.

"I've got to go."

Six days I'd been in one place, defenseless. I didn't know how I'd come to be there or why, but I knew that the longer I stayed, the closer the Circle would be to finding me. I had to leave. And soon.

The Mother Superior, however, didn't seem very concerned about ancient terror organizations. She had the look of a woman who might tell ancient terror organizations to bring it on.

"You will sit," she spat in heavily accented English.

"I'm sorry, Mother Superior," I said, my voice still raw. But the clock was ticking, and I couldn't stay any longer. Summer. I'd given myself until the end of the summer to follow in my father's footsteps, and I didn't dare waste a minute more.

"I am grateful to you and the sisters. If you will give me your name and an address, I'll send you money . . . payment for your services and—"

"We do not want your money. We want you to *sit*."

"If you could direct me to the train station—"

"There is no train station," the Mother Superior snapped. "Now, sit."

"I can't sit down! I have to leave! Now!" I looked around the small, crowded room. I was wearing a cotton nightgown that wasn't my own, and I clutched at it with bloody fingers. "I need my clothes and shoes, please."

"You don't have any shoes," Mary said. "When we found you, you were barefoot."

I didn't want to think about what that meant. I just looked at the innocent faces and tried to ignore the evil that might have followed me to their door.

"I need to leave," I said slowly, searching the Mother Superior's eyes. "It would be best if I left . . . now."

"Impossible," the Mother Superior said, then turned to the sisters. *"Wenn das Mädchen denkt daß wir sie in den Schnee rausgehen lassen würden, dann ist sie verrückt."*

My hands shook. My lips quivered. I know how I must have looked, because my new friend, Mary, was reaching for me, easing closer. "Don't you go worrying, now. You aren't in any trouble. The Mother Superior just said—"

"Snow." I pulled aside a curtain, looked out on a vast expanse of white, and whispered against the frosty glass, "She said *snow*."

"Oh, that's nothing." Mary took the curtain from me, sliding it back to block the chill. "These parts of the Alps are very high, you see. And, well, we've just had a bit of an early spell."

I jerked away from the window. "How early?" I asked, silently chanting to myself, *It is June. It is June. It is—*

"Tomorrow is the first of October."

"I . . . I think I'm going to be sick."

Mary grabbed me by the arm and helped me limp down the hall, past crucifixes and frosty windows to a bathroom with a cold stone floor.

I retched, but my stomach was empty except for the glass of water, my throat filled with nothing but sand. And still I heaved, throwing up the bile and acid that seemed to be eating away at my core.

When I closed my eyes, my head felt like a top, spinning in a place without gravity. When I finally pulled myself to my feet and leaned against the bathroom sink, a light flickered on, and I found myself staring into a face I totally didn't know. I would have jumped if I'd had the strength, but as it was, all I could do was lean closer.

My hair had been shoulder length and dishwater blond my whole life, but right then it was a little past my ears and as black as night. I pulled the nightgown over my head, felt my hair stand on end from the static, and stared at a body I no longer knew.

My ribs showed through my skin. My legs seemed longer, leaner. Bruises covered my knees. Red welts circled my wrists. Thick bandages covered most of one arm. But it all paled in comparison to the knot on the side of my head. I touched it gently, and the pain was so sharp that I thought I would be sick again, so I gripped the sink, leaned close to the mirror, and stared at the stranger in my skin.

"What did you do?"

Everything in my training told me that this was not the time to panic. I had to think, to plan. I thought of all the places I could go, but my mind drifted, wondering about the places I had been. When I moved, the pain shot through one ankle and up my leg, and I knew I would have a hard time running off that mountain.

"Here, here," Mary said, pressing a cool rag to my head. She brought a cup to my lips, made me drink, and then I whispered, "Why did you call me Gillian?"

"It was what you kept saying, over and over," she said. Her Irish accent seemed thicker in the small space. "Why? Isn't that your name?"

"No. I'm Cammie. Gilly is the name of . . . my sister."

"I see."

My mind swirled with the options of the things I should and shouldn't do until it finally settled on the only question that mattered.

"Mary, is there a telephone?"

Mary nodded. "The Mother Superior bought a satellite phone last summer."

Summer.

At the Gallagher Academy for Exceptional Young Women, there are typically seventy-six days in our summer vacation. That's eleven weeks. Just under three months. One quarter of a year. I had allowed myself the summer to search and hunt and hopefully find the truth about why the Circle wanted me. The season had never seemed that long before, but right then it was like a black hole, threatening to suck up everything in my life.

"Mary," I said, gripping the sink tighter and leaning into the light, "there's someone I need to call."

Chapter two

I can't say for certain, but I've got to admit that if this whole spy thing doesn't work out, I might seriously consider joining a convent. Really, when you think about it, it's not that different from life at the Gallagher Academy for Exceptional Young Women.

You've got old stone walls and an ancient sisterhood, a collection of women who feel the same calling and are all working toward a higher purpose. Oh, and neither place gives you a whole lot of say on your wardrobe.

At noon the next day, the Mother Superior said that I could have a pair of shoes, and the sisters lent me a coat. The clothes Mary laid on my bed were clean and neatly mended, but they seemed entirely too small.

"I'm sorry but . . . I don't think these will fit."

"They ought to," Mary said with a giggle. "They're yours."

Mine.

I fingered the soft cotton pants and old sweatshirt I would

have sworn I'd never seen before. The clothes were worn, lived in, and I didn't let myself think about all the living I could no longer remember doing.

"There," Mary said, watching me tie the drawstring on the pants that fit my new body perfectly. "I bet you feel just like your old self, now, don't ya?"

"Yes," I said, and Mary smiled at me so sweetly that I almost felt guilty for the lie.

They told me I should rest, that I needed my strength and my sleep, but I didn't want to wake up again and find it was past Christmas, New Year's, that my eighteenth birthday had come and gone without my knowledge; so instead I went outside.

As I stepped onto the small path that led to the convent door, I knew it was October, but I was unprepared to feel the chill. Snow covered everything. The branches of the trees were heavy overhead, snapping under the weight of the wet white clumps, crashing through the forest. They made a noise that was too loud—like rifle shots in the cold, thin air. I jumped at every sound and shadow, and I honestly didn't know which was worse—that I couldn't remember the last four months, or that for the first time in my life I had absolutely no idea which way was north. I kept the convent safely in my sight, terrified of going too far, not knowing how much more lost I could possibly be.

"We found you there." Mary must have followed me, because when I turned, she was behind me. Her strawberry hair was blowing free from her habit as she stood there, staring at a river that raged at the bottom of a rocky, steep ravine. She pointed to the bank. "On the big rock near that fallen tree."

"Was I awake?" I asked.

"Barely." Mary shoved her hands into her pockets and shivered. "When we found you, you were mumbling. Talking crazy."

"What did I say?" I asked. Mary started shaking her head, but something about me must have told her that I wasn't going to rest until I knew, because she took a deep breath.

"'It's true,'" the girl said, and shivered again in a way that I knew had nothing to do with the chill. "You said, *It's true*. And then you passed out in my arms."

There is something especially cruel about irony. I could recite a thousand random facts about the Alps. I could tell you the average precipitation and identify a half dozen edible plants. I knew so many things about those mountains in that moment—everything but how I'd reached them.

Mary studied the river below and then turned her gaze to me. "You must be a strong swimmer."

"I am," I said, but, skinny and weak as I was, Mary seemed to doubt it. She nodded slowly and turned back to the banks.

"The river is highest in the spring. That's when the snow melts, and the water is so fast—it's like the river's angry. It scares me. I won't go near it. In the winter, everything freezes, and the water's barely a trickle, all rocks and ice." She looked at me and nodded. "You're lucky you fell when you did. Any other time of year and you would have died for sure."

"Lucky," I repeated to myself.

I didn't know if it was altitude, or fatigue, or the sight of the mountains that loomed around us, but it was harder than it should have been to breathe.

"How far is the nearest town?"

"There's a small village at the base of that ridge." Mary turned and pointed, but her voice was not much more than a whisper when she said, "It's a long way down the mountain."

Maybe it was the way she stared into the distance, but for the first time, I realized I probably wasn't the only one who had run away from someone. Something. In my professional opinion, the Alps are an excellent place for hiding.

I turned back to the river, scanned the rocky shore and the waters that ran to the valleys below. "Where did I come from?" I whispered.

Mary shook her head and said, "God?"

It was as good a guess as any.

Standing there among the trees and mountains, the river and snow, I knew that I'd climbed almost to the top of the earth. The bruises and blood, however, told me I'd had a long, long fall.

"Who are you, Cammie?" Mary asked me. "Who are you really?"

And then I said maybe the most honest thing I'd ever uttered. "I'm just a girl who's ready to go home."

No sooner had I spoken the words than a dull sound rang through the air, drowning out the rushing of the river below. It was a rhythmic, pulsing noise, and Mary asked, "What is that?"

I looked up through the swirling snow to the black shadow in the cloudless sky.

"That's my ride."

Chapter tHReE

I know most girls think their mothers are the most beautiful women in the world. Most girls *think* that, but I'm the only one who's right. And yet there was something different about the woman who ran toward me, crouching beneath the chopper's spinning blades. Snow swirled, and the Alps seemed to shudder, but Rachel Morgan wasn't just my mom in that moment. She wasn't just my headmistress. She was a spy on a mission, and that mission . . . was me.

She didn't hesitate or slow; she just threw her arms around me and said, "You're alive." She squeezed tighter. "Thank God, you're alive." Her hands were strong and warm, and it felt like I might never leave her grasp again. "Cammie, what happened?"

"I left," I said, despite how obvious and silly it must have sounded.

Mary was gone, standing with the rest of the sisters, watching the chopper and the reunion from afar. My mother and I were alone as I explained, "People were getting hurt because of me, so I left to find out what the Circle wants from me. I had to find out what happened to Dad—what he knew. What they think *I* know. So I left." I gripped my mother's arms tighter, searched her eyes.

"Yesterday I woke up here."

Mom's hands were wrapped around the back of my neck—her fingers tangled in my hair—holding me steady.

"I know, sweetheart. I know. But now I need you to tell me everything you remember."

The chopper blades were spinning, but the whole world was standing still as I told her, *"I just did."*

Number of hours I slept on the trip back to Virginia: 7

Number of hours the trip actually took: 9

Number of croissants my mother tried to get me to eat: 6

Number of croissants I actually ate: 2 (The rest I wrapped in a napkin and saved for later.)

Number of questions anyone asked me: 1

Number of dirty looks my mother gave to prevent the question-asking: 37*

*estimated number, due to the aforementioned sleepiness

"Cam." My mother shook my shoulder, and I felt myself sinking lower in the sky. "We're here."

I would have known that sight anywhere—the black asphalt of Highway 10, the huge stone building on the horizon, surrounded by the high walls and electrified gates that served to shield my sisterhood from prying eyes. I knew that place and those things better than anything else in the world, and yet something felt strange as the helicopter flew across the forest. The trees were ablaze with bright reds and vivid yellows—colors that had no place at the beginning of summer.

"What is it, kiddo?"

"Nothing." I forced a smile. "It's nothing."

Of course, if you're reading this, you probably already know a lot about the Gallagher Academy; but there's a fact about my sisterhood that never makes it into the briefings. The truth of the matter is that, yes, we have been training covert operatives since 1865, but the thing that no one realizes until they've seen our school for themselves is this: we are a school for *girls*.

Seriously. In so many ways, we are just girls. We laugh with our friends and worry about our hair and wonder what boys are thinking. Sure, we do some of that wondering in Portuguese, but we're still girls just the same. In that way, the people in the town of Roseville understand us better than almost all the people at the CIA.

And believe me, it wasn't the spies-in-training I was nervous to see—it was the girls. But as the chopper landed and my mother opened the door, I knew it wasn't possible to avoid them.

Most of the freshman class stood halfway between the side doors and the Protection and Enforcement barn. An entire class of girls I'd never seen before stood huddled around Madame Dabney, who, I could have sworn, wiped a tear from an eye when I stepped onto the lawn. For a second, it felt as if my entire sisterhood were there, watching. And then the crowd parted to reveal a narrow path and three faces I knew better than my own.

"Oh my gosh!" Liz screamed, running toward me. She seemed even smaller than usual, her hair even blonder and straighter. I threw my arms around her, knowing I was home.

Then I felt a hand reach out to touch my hair. "That dye job is going to give you split ends, you know."

I did know. And I didn't care. But no sooner had I reached for Macey McHenry than she pushed away, held me at arm's length.

"What did you do to yourself?" she said, looking me up and down. "You look like death."

Which was exactly how I felt, but it didn't seem like the right time to say so. Everyone was watching, staring, waiting for . . . something. I wasn't sure what. So I just said, "It's good to see you, Macey." I smiled, but then something occurred to me. "Of course, it feels like I just saw you, but . . ."

I trailed off. I didn't want to talk about how my head was way more broken than my body, so I turned to my third and final roommate.

"Bex!" I yelled at the girl who stood a little apart from the others, arms crossed. She wasn't crying (like Liz) or cringing at my appearance (like Macey). She didn't even push closer, trying to get some kind of scoop (like Tina Walters). Rebecca Baxter just stood looking at me as if she wasn't entirely sure how she felt about seeing me in my current condition. Or maybe, I had to admit, about seeing me at all.

"Bex," I said, hobbling closer. "I'm back. Sorry I didn't bring you anything." I forced a laugh. "I must have lost my wallet."

I wanted it to be funny—I needed it to be funny because I couldn't shake the feeling that if she didn't laugh then I might cry.

"Bex, I—" I started, but Bex just turned to my mother.

"Welcome back, headmistress." She gave my mom a nod, and a look I didn't recognize passed between them. "They're waiting."

"Who's waiting?" The words echoed in the empty foyer as I followed my mother across the threshold of our school. For the first time in days, I had my bearings, and yet I still felt totally out of my depth. My internal clock must have reset itself somewhere over the Atlantic, because even before the crowd of girls began rushing through the door and down the halls, I knew that it was time to get back to class, to lab. To life. But I had absolutely no idea where that walk would lead me.

"Where are we going?" I asked. "What's going on?"

Liz walked beside me, but it was Macey who shrugged her shoulders and said, "Haven't you heard, Cam? You're an international incident."

But neither my mother nor Bex said a thing. A moment later, Mr. Smith (or someone I assumed was Mr. Smith since he always gets massive plastic surgery over the summer) fell into step beside us. "How was it, Rachel?" he asked.

Mom nodded. "Like we thought." She took a piece of Evapopaper from him, scanned the contents, and dropped it into a small fountain, where it instantly dissolved. "The team's on the ground?"

"Yes," Professor Buckingham said, walking down the Grand Staircase and joining us. "They've scanned the area around the convent, but as soon as Cameron escaped, the Circle would have abandoned the—"

"Keep looking. Somebody had to see something."

"Rachel." Buckingham's voice was no louder than a whisper, and yet it stopped my mother in her tracks. "The area is incredibly remote. We don't even know that she was being held *on* the mountain. She could have escaped from a transport or . . . Rachel, they're gone."

I expected Mom to climb the stairs, to walk through the Hall of History and to her office, but she turned instead and started for the small hallway behind the Grand Stairs, Buckingham and Mr. Smith at her side.

"What else?" Mom asked.

"Well," Mr. Smith said cautiously, "we think she should begin with a full battery of neurological tests."

"After we debrief her," Mom said.

"She'll need a full physical workup as well," Mr. Smith added. "We can't expect her to return to class if she's not—"

"*She* is right here!"

I hadn't meant to yell—I really hadn't. They were the last people in the world I would ever want to disrespect, but I couldn't stand hearing them talk about me like I was still lost on the other side of the world.

"I'm here," I said, softer.

"Of course you are." Professor Buckingham patted my arm and turned to stare into a mirror that hung in the narrow hallway. A thin red line spread across her face, and in the reflection, I saw the eyes of the painting behind us flash green. A split second later the mirror was sliding aside, revealing a small elevator, which I knew would take us to Sublevel One.

"We're very glad to have you home, Cameron," Buckingham said with another pat. She stepped inside, along with Mr. Smith. Bex started to follow, but Mom blocked the way.

"You girls can go to class now. Cammie will catch up with you after she's been debriefed and examined."

"But . . ." Bex started.

"Go to class," Mom said. But they didn't really trust me to leave their sight again, I could tell; and Mom must have known it, because she moved inside the car without me.

"Cammie, I'll see you downstairs in a minute," she said, and the doors slid closed.

For the first time in months, my three best friends and I were alone. How many hours had we spent walking those halls together in the early morning or middle of the night? Sneaking. Planning. Testing our limits and ourselves. But standing there, we were all a little too straight—our posture a little too perfect. It was as if we were strangers trying to make a good impression.

"Stop looking at me like that," I told them when it finally became too much.

"Like how?" Liz asked.

"Like you didn't think you'd ever see me again," I said.

"Cam, we—" Liz started, but Bex cut her off.

"You don't get it, do you?" Her voice was more hiss than whisper. "Until forty-eight hours ago, we didn't."

Chapter foUR

The first time I'd ever seen the elevator to Sublevel One, I'd been starting my sophomore year. Real-life fieldwork had seemed ages away. Covert Operations was a totally new subject. And Bex was my best friend. As the car began to sink into the top secret depths of my school, I had to wonder if *all* of those things had changed. I didn't want to think about the way Bex had looked at me. I didn't want to cry. So I just stood there wondering if anything was ever going to be the same again, when the doors slid open and my mother said, *"Follow me."*

There's a tone of voice that adults get that lets you know that you're in trouble. I heard it then, and suddenly I wanted back on the chopper. Sadly, running away a second time seemed like a terrible idea, so I had no choice but to turn and follow my mother inside the room where I'd learned my first lessons in Covert Operations. But with one glance I knew it wasn't a classroom anymore. Right then, it was a war room.

A long table sat in the middle of the space, chairs all around it. There were phones and computers, a massive screen that showed an aerial image of the convent and the mountain. I smelled burned coffee and stale doughnuts. For a second, I was tempted to close my eyes and imagine that I was just another part of the team.

But then a chair squeaked, and Madame Dabney asked, "How are you, Cameron?" and I had to remember that when you go to spy school, some questions are way more complicated than they appear.

Say "I'm okay," and you might sound like an idiot who doesn't care she has amnesia.

Say "I'm terrified," and risk looking like a wimp or a coward.

"My head hurts" sounds like a whiner.

"I just want to go to bed" sounds like someone too foolish or lazy to care about the truth.

But saying nothing to the faculty of the Gallagher Academy for Exceptional Young Women wasn't exactly an option either, so I took the seat at the opposite end of the table, looked my teachers squarely in the eyes, and told them, "I'm feeling better, thank you."

It must have been the right answer, because Madame Dabney smiled in my direction. "Do you feel like answering some questions for us?"

"Yes," I said, even though what I needed was to have questions answered for me. Collectively, they'd probably been on a thousand different missions in their lifetimes, and I knew they'd combed the corners of the earth to find out what had happened over the summer. I wanted to know everything they'd discovered, and so much more.

Madame Dabney smiled. "Why don't you begin by telling us why you ran away?"

"I didn't run away," I said, louder than I'd intended. "I left." My mind drifted back to the night when the Circle cornered me in the middle of a mountain, and the look on Joe Solomon's face as he triggered the explosion that, in so many ways, was still reverberating through my life. "Mr. Solomon was willing to die to save me. People were getting hurt because of me, and . . . I knew that I wasn't *in* danger." I looked down at my hands. "I *was* the danger."

I sat waiting for someone to tell me I was wrong. I wanted them to say that the Circle had started this and the Circle alone was to blame, but those words never came. Being right had never been so disappointing.

Professor Buckingham was the only one who moved, and she leaned closer. "Cameron, listen to me." Her voice was like granite, and the Circle seemed almost soft in comparison. "What is the last thing you remember?"

"Writing my report and leaving it in the Hall of History."

Buckingham picked up a bound manuscript and placed it on the table in front of me. "This report?"

It looked different from the loose pages I'd left on top of the case with Gilly's sword months before, but that was it. I knew it. So I nodded. "I was in a hurry to finish it. I had to put everything down so I could . . . leave."

Buckingham smiled as if that made perfect sense. "Do *you* know where you went?"

As soon as Buckingham spoke, my mother gave her a look. It was nothing more than a glance, really, but something in the gesture made me say, "What? Do you know something?"

"It's nothing, kiddo." Mom reached for my hand, covered it with her own, and squeezed my fingers. They were still raw and red, but they didn't really hurt. "We just need you to start at the beginning. We need you to tell us if you know where you went when you left."

I closed my eyes and tried to think, but the halls of my memory were black and empty.

"I don't . . . I'm sorry. I don't know."

"What about later?" Buckingham asked. "Any flashes or scenes . . . feelings? It could be anything. Any little thing might be important."

"No." I shook my head. "Nothing. I left the report and then I woke up in the convent."

"Cameron, dear." Madame Dabney sounded very disappointed. "You were gone for four months. You don't remember anything?"

It should have been an easy question for a Gallagher Girl. I'd been trained to remember and recall. I knew what we'd had for lunch on the last day of finals, and I could tell from the way she was sitting that Professor Buckingham's bad hip was giving her trouble—that it was probably going to rain. I knew Madame Dabney had changed perfumes, and Mr. Smith had used his favorite plastic surgeon—the one in Switzerland—to rework his face last summer. But my own summer was a total blank.

My head hurt, and in the back of my mind a song began to play, lulling me. I wanted to sway with the music.

"I'm sorry," I told them. "I know it sounds crazy. *I* sound crazy. I wouldn't blame you if you didn't believe me."

"You are many things, Cameron. But crazy is not one of them." Buckingham straightened. "We believe you."

I expected them to push harder, demand more. But then Buckingham took off her glasses and picked up the papers on the table in front of her. "The medical staff is expecting you in the infirmary, Cameron." I'd thought I'd been good at hiding my fatigue, but the smile she gave me said otherwise. "And then I do hope you'll get some rest. I think you've earned it."

Walking back through the gleaming corridors of Sublevel One, I felt my mother's hand on my back, and something about that small gesture made me stop.

"I'll remember, Mom," I blurted, turning to her. "I'll get better and I'll fight this and I'll remember. And then—"

"No," Mom snapped, then lowered her voice. "No, Cammie. I do not want you picking at your memories like they're some kind of scab. Scabs exist for a reason."

"But—" I started, just as Mom reached for my shoulders, held me tight.

"Listen to me, Cammie. There are things in this life . . . in this world . . . There are things that you don't *want* to remember."

The other teachers were on the far side of a soundproof

door, halfway down the hall, and I couldn't help wondering if Mom would have said those things in front of them. Somehow I knew this wasn't the advice of a senior operative; this was the warning of a mother.

"But I need to know."

"No." She shook her head and cupped my face. "You don't."

When she touched me this time, I suddenly realized that I wasn't the only one who was thinner. I wasn't the only one whose hair had lost its natural shine. I'd seen her look that way only once before—when we'd lost my father. And right then it dawned on me—I had lost my memories, but . . . last summer . . . my mother had lost me.

"Mom, I'm sorry." I could feel myself wanting to cry, but the tears didn't come. "I'm so, so sorry I made you worry. I was going to come back. I was going to come back so much sooner."

"I don't care about that."

"You don't?" I asked, certain that I had misheard her.

"I care that you are home. I care that you are safe. I care that this is over. Sweetheart"—she smoothed my hair away from the terrible lump that was still tender—"just let it be over."

"Rachel." Mr. Smith was standing in the doorway, waving my mother back into the room. But Mom ignored him and kept staring at me.

"Promise me, Cammie, that you will *let this be over*."

"I . . . I promise."

She pulled back and wiped her eyes. "Can you find your way upstairs?"

"Yes, I remember." I didn't think about the words. "I mean . . ." I started, but then trailed off, because my mother had already turned. My mother was already gone.

From the moment I'd awoken at the convent, one of the nuns had always been by my side. Since my mother had landed in Austria, I'd barely left her sight. So it felt more than a little strange walking alone through the empty corridor that led to the Gallagher Academy hospital wing.

I was finally alone.

But that was before I turned the corner and saw a boy standing in the center of the hall.

His hands hung loosely by his sides, and his hair was neatly combed. His white shirt and khaki pants were clean and freshly pressed. At a glance I might have confused him with just an ordinary private school boy. But, 1) There *are* no boys at my school. And 2) Zachary Goode has never been ordinary a day in his life.

I stood motionless. Waiting. Trying to reconcile the fact that Zach was there, standing in the middle of my school, looking at me like maybe I was the one who was totally out of place. He reached out one hand, his finger sliding down my arm as if to check to make sure I was real, and the touch made me close my eyes, waiting for his lips to find mine, but they never did.

"Zach," I said, easing closer. "What are you doing here? Are you . . . ? Is it . . . ?" The questions didn't matter, so the words didn't come. "You're here!"

"Funny, I was about to say the same about you."

Just to reiterate: I was alone. With Zach. In my school.

Crazy was taking on a whole new meaning.

"What are you doing here?" I asked.

"I sort of . . . go . . . here now."

"You do?" I asked, then nodded, the facts settling down around me. Zach's mother was a prominent member of the Circle. The fact that he had chosen to work against her meant that the same people who were after me were after him. The Gallagher Academy was one of the safest places on earth—probably *the* safest school. It made sense that he would come back and enroll full-time after the summer.

"Cammie," a woman behind me said. "I'm Dr. Wolf. We're ready for you."

I knew I was supposed to turn—to go take their tests, answer their questions, and start trying to unravel the mystery of my mind—but I just stood, feeling Zach's fingers play with the ends of my hair.

"How . . . are you?" I managed to mutter.

"It's different," he said, looking at my new short locks as if he hadn't heard my question at all. "It's different now."

Chapter five

Over the course of the next four hours, there were nine tests and three doctors. I spent thirty minutes strapped inside a metal tube, listening to a mechanic whirring so loud I couldn't even hear myself think. They X-rayed every part of my body, scanned every part of my mind. I leaned against a metal brace, squinted into a light, and recited all the prime numbers between one and a thousand in Japanese.

I kept waiting for words like *concussion* or *trauma*, but there was nothing but hasty scribbling on notepads. The doctors' expressions didn't betray a single thing. They were all Gallagher grads, after all. Their poker faces stayed as blank as my memory.

"Well, Cammie," Dr. Wolf said, after I'd changed into clean clothes, "how are you feeling?"

"Fine," I said, relieved that at least my lying ability had made it through the summer intact.

"Dizziness?" she asked, and gave me knowing look.

"Some," I admitted.

"Nausea?"

"Yes," I said.

"Headaches?" she guessed, and I nodded. "These things are normal, Cammie. That's quite a bump you've got there." She pointed to the knot on my head.

"What is it, Cammie?" the doctor asked when I didn't say anything, reading me as clearly as if I were still hooked up to one of her machines.

"You've seen my file?"

"Of course," she said with a nod.

"Well, it's just that I've been hit on the head a lot in the past," I told her. "I mean *a lot* a lot."

The woman nodded and raised an eyebrow. "I know. That's quite a bad habit you've got there."

I wanted to laugh at the joke, to smile, to do as my mother asked and just let it be over, but all I could do was search the doctor's eyes and say the thing that, until then, I hadn't admitted to a single soul. *"This feels different."*

"Does it?" the doctor asked.

Sitting there in only a tank top and shorts, I felt naked as I said, "Yes."

"I see."

The doctor placed a hand on my shoulder and answered the question I hadn't quite had the strength to ask. "If your memory comes back, Cammie, it will be on its own time. It will be when you are *ready*. Now, why don't you go get settled in? I'll tell the kitchen to send a tray to your room. You should try to get some sleep." Dr. Wolf smiled. "You'll feel better in the morning."

I hadn't forgotten my mother's words—my mother's warning—but in spite of them, I had to ask, "Is there anything I can do . . . to make myself remember?"

"You can rest, Cammie." Dr. Wolf smiled. "And you can wait."

Waiting. Like it or not, it's a skill all spies have to master eventually.

Walking through the halls, I closed my eyes and tried to test my memory. I knew there was a squeaky floorboard on my right and a nick in the base of the bookshelf on my left. I could have made it all the way to my room like that, eyes closed, memory guiding my way. Everything felt and sounded and smelled so familiar that the convent seemed a million miles away—like it had happened to some other girl.

But then I heard the music.

It was coming from the west, I was certain, filling the corridor. Soft and low but too clear to be a figment of my mind.

It was *real*, the notes clear and strong and drifting through the hall.

It was almost like a waltz, but I didn't want to dance.

It sounded like an old-fashioned organ. But there were no organs in the mansion. Or at least I didn't think there were. All I knew for certain was that, right then, the pain in my ankle subsided; my head stopped swirling, and I followed the sound until it was suddenly replaced by the opening of a door and heavy footsteps. Voices.

"I can't go to the room. *She'll* be there."

It was Bex, but the tone was one I'd never heard before. I hated it. And, most of all, I hated how sure I was that "she" was me.

I felt myself creeping closer to the cracked door, and peeking into the nearly abandoned classroom, listening as Zach told her, "You're going to have to talk to her eventually."

"I can't do it," Bex said.

Zach laughed. "I find that hard to believe. I'm the guy who was with you and your parents all summer, remember? *I* was in Budapest. I saw you in action in Greece. So don't pull that on me. I know exactly what you're capable of."

"Budapest was an exception," she told him, but then she laughed too. She was sitting next to him on top of a desk, her bare leg pressing against his khakis, and I thought I might be sick.

"What about Macey and Liz?" Zach asked.

"They think we have to act like nothing's wrong—that we have to pretend so maybe she'll get her memory back or whatever."

My breath was coming so hard I feared it might betray me as I stood there realizing that Liz and Macey had been pretending. Pretending *what*, I didn't know. Not to hate me? To be happy I was home? That my mother was right and it was over? Whatever it was, they were good at it. Bex, evidently, wasn't even going to bother.

"She looks so different," Zach said, and Bex leaned against his shoulder, closed her eyes.

"She *is* different," Bex said.

And then, despite everything I'd been through, I wanted to forget what I was hearing. What I was seeing. Amnesia seemed like a welcome release, so I turned as quickly and quietly as I could and rushed back the way I'd come.

Halfway down the hall, I heard a door slam. Zach and Bex were in the hall behind me, talking and coming close. So I pushed down a narrow corridor, groping for a light fixture I'd first discovered in the seventh grade, praying it would still work, just as the bookshelf in front of me slid aside and I darted through the opening, disappearing into the dark.

Here's the thing you need to know about secret passageways; they're . . . well . . . secret, so that means they don't exactly get cleaned. Ever. At the Gallagher Academy, I was the only one who used them, and I'd been gone for months. The bookcase closed behind me, blocking Bex and Zach away; but I had to keep moving, so I pushed farther and farther down the dusty corridor until I realized . . . Wait.

It wasn't dusty.

Usually in the first weeks of school, my uniforms were covered with grime, my hair full of cobwebs. But that narrow passage was totally free of all the things that were supposed to be there—no dust or spiders, just a well-worn path that led to a door that I had never seen before.

For a second, I wondered if my memory of the mansion was

as broken as my memory of the summer, and I stood listening for a long time. There were only the faintest sounds of humming and beeping, so I took a deep breath and opened the door, steadied my nerves, and stepped inside.

There was a couch and a cushy chair, some flowers in a vase. Curtains hung from the ceiling in the center of the room. I eased forward, pulled them aside, and looked down at Joe Solomon, who lay perfectly still on a bed.

His bruises had faded, and the stitches were gone. The burns he'd sustained in the explosion at the Blackthorne Institute last spring were almost entirely mended—nothing but a few almost unnoticeable scars. My favorite teacher looked like he was just sleeping and might wake up at any moment, tell me that my vacation was over, and I was going to need my strength for whatever he had planned for CoveOps the next morning.

"I'm home, Mr. Solomon," I said, easing forward. "I'm back."

But the only reply was the sound of the machines that buzzed and beeped. The room was an eerie kind of quiet. I leaned down and kissed the top of his head, enjoying the company of the one person who wasn't mad that I'd left and even madder that I'd been so late in coming back.

Standing there holding Joe Solomon's hand, I heard the music in my mind again, louder. Clearer. And all of a sudden I couldn't think of anything else—not Bex or Zach, not the Circle or the convent.

The couch was just a few feet away, and it felt good to finally sit—to rest. If Mr. Solomon said anything, I didn't hear it. I was already fast asleep.

Chapter Six

"**H**ello, sleepyhead."

I jolted awake in the dim room. My neck hurt and my eyes burned, and it took a moment for me to realize that whoever was speaking, she wasn't talking to me.

"There are waffles for breakfast, Joe. Do you remember that little place outside Belfast? What was its name? The cook had a crush on you, and she'd make waffles every morning even though they weren't on the menu."

I watched my aunt Abby sink into the chair next to Mr. Solomon's bed, reach for my teacher's hand just like I'd done the night before.

"What was the name, Joe? Wake up and tell me it's sloppy of me not to remember the name."

She wasn't asking—she was pleading. She sat for a second, waiting for an answer that never came. Then she leaned closer and straightened the blanket that covered his legs.

"Cam's home, Joe," she said. "She's back. Of course, you

know already know that, don't you? Because even in here you know everything." She gave a quick, easy laugh. "Well . . . that and because she's sitting right behind me."

The thing you need to know about Abigail Cameron is that not only is she an awesome operative, but also, when her hair is down and the light is right and she spins around like she did that morning, she kind of looks like the star of a shampoo commercial. Her eyes didn't carry the shocked relief of my mother's. Her face was totally missing the detached anger of my friends. There was nothing but pure happiness in her when she looked at me and shrugged.

"What? No *hello* for your favorite aunt?"

It sounded like she was teasing—she *looked* like she was teasing. But my homecoming so far had been so totally not tease-worthy, that I guess I just sat there feeling dumbstruck.

"So . . . were you ever going to say hello?" Abby asked with a pout. "I thought I wasn't even going to see you until class."

"Class?"

"Oh, yeah." She smiled. "I'm your Covert Operations teacher, didn't you hear? And I have to say I kind of rock at it. Of course"—she turned back to the bed, leaned close to Mr. Solomon—"I only agreed to fill in until this guy decides to go back to work."

She was daring him, taunting him, challenging him to wake up and say otherwise, but it didn't happen. Joe Solomon wasn't going to be dared into doing anything, and Abby gave a sigh as if deep down she knew it.

"I didn't know," I told her. "I mean, if I had known, I would have come to see you, but I didn't. I found this room last night when the doctors were finished with me, and then I saw Mr. Solomon and . . . I must have fallen asleep."

"We knew where you were, Cam." All the tease was gone from her voice. "From this point on, we will always know where you are."

It was harder to look at her then, so I looked at Mr. Solomon.

"Is he . . . better?"

"He's stable." Abby smoothed his hair and pinched his cheek. "Isn't he a cutie when he's sleeping?" she asked, and leaned closer. "Get mad, Joe. Roll over and tell me to shut up. Do it."

"Has he been here the whole time?"

Abby nodded. "We have everything we need to care for him. Dr. Fibs spent the whole summer developing a device that will keep his muscles from atrophying. Our medical staff is able to monitor his condition far more closely than a regular hospital would. And, of course, it's significantly safer. Plus"—she smoothed the blankets—"everyone he loves is here."

I thought of the way my mother had sat for days at his bedside, holding his bandaged hands. *Everyone he loves.*

"Who knows that he's . . ."

"Not dead? Or not really a double agent working for the Circle of Cavan?" Abby guessed, but then she seemed to realize that the two questions would have the exact same answer. "As few people as possible. The academy faculty, of course. Bex's parents. Agent Townsend—you know he had the nerve to send me a class syllabus?" She gave a short, mocking laugh. "*He* gave *me* notes for a proper course of study for young ladies in the clandestine services," she said in a spot-on English accent.

It sounded just like the man I'd met last spring, and I had to laugh. Then, just that quickly, I had to stop. It felt wrong, there, in Joe Solomon's hospital room, with my missing summer looming like a shadow in the back of my mind.

"I'm sorry, Aunt Abby. I'm sorry for . . . everything."

"I'm not." She reached for the dead flowers in the vase by the bed and threw them in the trash. "Oh, I could have killed you if I'd gotten my hands on you a week ago, but now . . ."

"You're glad to see me?" I tried to guess, but my aunt gave a shake of her head.

"Now we're just glad you're home."

Maybe it was the medicinal properties of a good night's sleep, or the power radiating off of my aunt, but I felt stronger, surer. And I forgot all about my mother's warning from the day before.

"Don't worry, Abby. I'll take all the tests and do all the exercises. I'll do the work—I'll do . . . anything. And I'll remember. I'll get my memory back and I'll—"

"Don't, Cammie." Abby was turning, shaking her head. "Just don't . . . push it."

"I'm ready to push it. I'm ready to work and . . . What?" There was something in her expression, a sort of hopeful peace as she gripped my hands and searched my eyes.

"Don't you see, Cammie? The Circle might have had you."

I heard my voice crack. "I know."

"So maybe *they got what they wanted*."

For almost a year I'd lived with the knowledge that the Circle getting what they wanted was a bad thing. But right then Abby was looking at me as if she didn't care about that.

"My mom said . . ." I choked and tried again. "Mom said I shouldn't try to remember."

"You shouldn't," Abby said.

"Why?"

"Cam, look at this." She gently turned my hand so that I had no choice but to see the long bandages that covered the gashes on my arm. "Do you know what makes marks like this?"

I wanted to scream that that was the point, but I stayed speechless.

Abby let my arm fall. "Do you really *want* to know?"

I thought about the marks and the words and the terror in my mother's eyes as she told me there are some things we don't want to remember.

"Torture?" I said, but it wasn't really a question. The answer was already there—in Abby's eyes and on my skin. They thought I'd been tortured.

"Whatever it was, Cam. Whatever you lived through, it's over. So maybe now the whole thing is over."

"You mean maybe the Circle doesn't want me anymore?"

Abby nodded slowly. She gripped my hands tighter. "Maybe now things can go back to normal."

Normal. I liked the sound of that. Sure, as the daughter of two secret agents, a student at a top secret and highly dangerous school (not to mention someone who'd spent more than a year as the target of an ancient terrorist organization), I didn't really know what normal meant, but that didn't matter. Normal was my new mission. Normal was the goal within my sights.

Unfortunately, as soon as I reached the Grand Hall, I realized that normal was also a moving target.

"Hi," Zach said, because, oh yeah, evidently Zach now had a regular place at our table in the Grand Hall. Then I looked up and down the crowded benches and realized that his new place was my old place.

"Hi," I said back to him, because, honestly, what else can you say in that situation? You can't really yell at your boyfriend for stealing your seat and your best friend. You also can't yell at your best friend for stealing your boyfriend. Or . . . you can . . . but *Hi* seemed like a much easier way to start the morning.

"Welcome back, Cam," Tina Walters said, after what seemed like forever.

"So what did you . . ." Eva Alvarez started, then stopped herself as if she'd already said the wrong thing. "I mean, did you have . . . Or . . . It's good to see you," she finally blurted.

"It's good to see you too, Eva." I forced a smile. "It's good to be back," I said, even though it totally felt like I had just left.

"Here." Liz pressed closer to Macey. Together, the two of them were about as wide as a regular person, so I was able to squeeze onto the bench.

"Thanks," I told her, pushing a few of her books aside, skimming over words like *neurosurgery* and *cognition*.

"Doing some light reading?" I asked.

41

Liz grabbed the books and shoved them into her backpack.

"You know, the brain is totally fascinating. Of course, it's a myth that we only use ten percent of our brain function."

"Of course *you* use more," Zach and Bex said at the same time. They gave almost identical laughs, and I flashed back to what I'd heard the night before. I saw the way Bex and Zach sat together on the other side of the table, and my head hurt for reasons that had nothing to do with blunt force trauma.

"So where were you?" Macey asked, looking at me over the top of Liz's head.

"Macey!" Liz hissed. "You know we're not supposed to bother Cam with questions. Her memory will return if and when she's ready." She sounded like she was quoting someone or something verbatim.

"Last night," Macey clarified, with a smirk in Liz's direction. "Where were you *last night*?"

"Hospital," I said, and risked a look at Zach and Bex—wondered what it would have been like to return to our suite after overhearing the two of them together. "I had to spend the night in a hospital room." (Totally not a lie.)

"Are you . . ." Liz started.

"I'm fine," I said, maybe too quickly. "Tests. They ran a bunch of tests."

"Good," Liz said with a decisive nod. "They did an MRI, didn't they? What about an EEG? PET scan? We really need to get a baseline assessment. The Barnes theory says that memory is—"

"That's enough, Liz," Bex said softly, and for a second, no one had anything to say.

Well, no one but Tina Walters.

Tina seemed exactly like her old self as she pushed aside a bowl of strawberry jam, leaned on the table, and lowered her voice. "Well, I heard that while they were looking for you, they found someone else."

She stopped and let the silence draw out. If she wanted someone to ask who it was, she was disappointed, but didn't show it as she whispered, *"Joe Solomon."*

Sure, Joe Solomon was two flights of stairs away, but judging by the looks on the majority of faces at the table, no one besides my roommates, Zach, and I seemed to know it.

Tina gestured with a piece of extra-crispy bacon. "He's alive and well and working for the Circle in South Africa." She took a bite. "Maybe he's the one who had you?" she asked, turning to me. "Or maybe the Circle kidnapped you, but Mr. Solomon is really a *triple* agent and he—"

"I don't know who was holding me, Tina," I said.

"Really," Tina started, "wouldn't that be something? Mr. Solomon out there. With you and—"

"I've heard enough." Bex stood, shaking her head.

"Bex—" I started, but she wheeled on me.

"What?" she snapped. "What do you have to say?"

It was a really good question. And I'm sure I totally had answers, but right then my reasons for leaving, for running, for chasing the Circle halfway around the world were gone, lost, like the rest of my memories. So I just sat, looking at my best friend in the world, and the only words that came to mind were "I'm sorry."

The look she gave me was one I'd never seen before. Was she mad or hurt, terrified or indignant? Bex is the most naturally gifted spy I know. Her eyes were impossible to read.

"Oh, Cameron, here you are!" Professor Buckingham's voice sliced through the crowded hall.

"Yeah," Bex said at last. "Here she is."

When Bex turned and left, I wanted to go after her, but Buckingham was standing too close for me to follow. Besides, despite everything, there was really nothing left to say.

"Cameron, you are, of course, responsible for any and all work you missed during your absence—none of which is insignificant during the Gallagher Academy's senior year."

Professor Buckingham cut her eyes at me, expecting me to argue, I guess, but all I could think was *senior year*. I don't know if it was the head trauma or the fatigue, but I hadn't really thought about the fact that I was a senior. I looked around at the girls who filled the hall, and for the first time it occurred to me that none of them were older than us, more trained than us, more ready than us for the outside world.

Even without the Circle, that fact would have terrified me.

"Now, if you don't feel up to the task quite yet—"

"No," I blurted, reaching for the course schedule in Professor Buckingham's hands. "I want to. I want to work—for things to get back to normal."

And I meant it—I really did. But then Buckingham turned and strolled toward the doors, past my best friends, who didn't know how to act around me, younger girls who were staring at me, and Zach—yes, Zach. Who was at my school. Who had spent the summer with my Bex. Who was sitting in the Grand Hall like he'd been there for years.

And I remembered "normal" might never be the same again.

Chapter Seven

I remember everything that happened that morning. Or, well, *almost* everything.

Madame Dabney talked for a long time about how lovely it was to have me back, and then she handed me a beautifully lettered condolence card on the loss of my memory. Mr. Smith had a lot of questions about the Alps and the nuns (one of whom he was pretty sure he might have dated during a bad operation on the Hungarian border in the early eighties).

Routine is good, the doctor had told me. My memory would come back if and when I was ready. So when Mr. Smith handed me a pop quiz from the week before, I told myself I'd only missed it because I'd been sick and confined to bed, and I didn't let myself obsess about the details.

At 10:20 exactly, the entire senior class grabbed their things and headed downstairs. When we reached the main floor, Liz and the rest of the girls on the research track peeled off and started for the labs in the basement. But at the last second, Liz stopped short.

"Bye, Cam." She looked afraid to let me out of her sight. "See you later?"

"Of course you will," Macey said, looping her arm through mine as if I couldn't possibly run away again on her watch.

"Yeah," I said. "I'll see you at lunch, Lizzie."

"Okay," Liz said, then turned and headed for the labs. She was almost gone before I realized that Macey was still beside me.

"Macey, don't you have to go with her?"

"Nope," she said, and flashed me a sly smile.

"But . . ." I started, my foggy mind doing the mental math, because even though she was our age, Macey had come late to the Gallagher Academy. Aside from one or two subjects, we'd never been in the same classes before.

"She caught up," Bex said, her voice frigid as she started down the dark hall behind the kitchen.

Students never went down there. There were no classrooms or cool places to study. The light was bad and sometimes the hallway smelled so much like onions that my eyes watered. I'd never—not in five years—seen Bex show any interest in that hallway, but she was disappearing down it as if she walked it every day.

"Hey, Bex!" Zach yelled. He barreled down the Grand Staircase, running after her. I don't think he even saw me as he fell into step with Bex, the two of them turning a corner, out of sight.

"Where are they going?"

I couldn't hide the bitterness in my voice, but Macey didn't seem to hear it. She just looked at me as if maybe I'd been knocked on the head even harder than she'd realized.

Her voice was full of mischief when she cocked a hip and said, *"Sublevel Three."*

Okay, not to sound braggy or anything, but after five full years, I was pretty sure I knew every part of the Gallagher Academy. I mean, seriously—*all the parts* (including the ones that got condemned due to an unfortunate uranium incident in 1967).

So I had a pretty good idea of what to expect. After all, Sublevel One was all research books and classrooms, massive training stations comprised of steel and glass and secrets. Sublevel Two was more like a maze—long spiraling corridors filled with our most precious artifacts and dangerous files. The first sublevel looked like something straight out of the future; the second looked like it had been ripped from the past. But as soon as the elevator opened into Sublevel Three, I knew I'd found my way into a place far older than the school itself.

Shadows and stone stretched before us. Dim, old-fashioned bulbs hung from a low ceiling. There was nothing but the sound of footsteps and the *drip-drip-drip* of falling water coming from somewhere I couldn't see. We weren't just in a different part of the mansion—it felt like we were in a different part of the world. And yet when I touched the wall, there was something so familiar about the feel of the stone beneath my fingers, the smell of the musty air.

"The classroom's this way." Macey started down a narrow hallway, and I followed slowly behind. But with every step, I found it harder and harder to breathe. My gut was telling me, *Run. Fight. Flee. Get out of here before it's too late, before—*

"It's okay, Cammie."

Zach was alone in the corridor behind me. How long he'd been standing there, I couldn't say, but it must have been long enough to know, or at least guess, what I'd been thinking, because he said, "You're not crazy."

"I'm not?" I asked, honestly not sure of the answer anymore.

"No." He shook his head, looked at the low stone ceiling and too-close walls. "It's just like the tombs."

I breathed in the musty air, and my mind flashed back to the cramped, abandoned tunnels that ran through the mountains that surrounded the Blackthorne Institute. There had been a time when I would have done almost anything to find out the secrets Zach had been hiding about his school, but a lot of things had changed during that fateful mission last semester.

The path was clear ahead of me. Only Zach blocked the way behind. And yet I couldn't move.

I just stood, staring. I didn't mention the fact that his mom had spent the last year trying to kidnap me.

It didn't seem like the time to ask why he'd never told me that Blackthorne was really a school for assassins.

All the things that had been weird the last time I'd seen him had just gotten weirder. I'd been running for months, for miles, but those unsaid things were still there, exactly where we'd left them.

"Cammie, we're in here," Abby yelled through a hole in the stone that could best be described as a doorway. So I turned and went inside.

I'd always suspected that my aunt Abby was the kind of woman who would be good at almost anything she tried. With one glance at her walking through the classroom, handing back old assignments, I could tell that teaching would be no different.

"I hope everyone enjoyed last week's little lesson in overt surveillance countermeasures. It's a very important subject, regardless of what Agent Townsend thinks," Aunt Abby added to the senior CoveOps class. "Ms. Walters, please remember that setting a suspected observation point on fire is effective but perhaps a little *too* overt in most cases."

Tina shrugged, and I looked around. *Classroom* didn't really seem like the right word to describe the space. It was more like a cave outfitted with long, tall tables, each with a pair of stools. I stood by the entrance, realizing there was no room at any of the tables for me.

"Come on up here, Cam." Abby pulled a stool from the corner and placed it behind the table at the very front of the class. "You can share with me."

Climbing onto that stool, I felt entirely too visible, conspicuous. It wasn't just the chameleon in me who wanted to hide. It was the Gallagher Girl who'd broken the rules, been foolish—gotten caught. I couldn't help feeling that Sublevel Three might spit me out because I hadn't earned the right to be there.

Then my aunt moved to the corner of the tall table and leaned against it, like I'd seen Joe Solomon do about a million times.

"Professor Townsend," she said, with a roll of her eyes, "suggested that this section of the curriculum be postponed—I don't think he even bothered to teach it to the seniors last year. Not that he taught anything else," she added under her breath. "But I say you need to know."

She walked to a corner of the room, picked up one of the wooden crates that were stacked there, carried it to the front table, and set it down beside me.

"I say it's time for you to know"—she held the crate by its ends and flipped it, sending at least a dozen objects skidding across the table—"about this."

There were springs and tubes, small cylinders I'd never seen before. The whole class leaned closer to get a better look—everyone but Zach, who didn't move, didn't stare.

"You know what this is, don't you?" Abby asked him.

He seemed almost ashamed when he said, "Yes."

"I thought so." There was no judgment in Abby's voice. "Do you feel like telling us about it?"

Zach shook his head. "No."

Abby looked as if she couldn't really blame him. "The Gallagher Academy takes protection and enforcement seriously. And for good reason," my aunt said, and I could have sworn that, for a split second, her gaze drifted to me. "But there are certain things we have not covered . . . until now." She stepped away from the table and moved closer to the rest of the class.

"These boxes contain long-range, high-powered rifles, and they are part of the most controversial topic that we will cover at this school. So why is that?" she asked, moving down the aisle, all eyes trained on her. "Why do people like Agent Townsend think you shouldn't be around"—she gestured to the weapon on the table—"*these*?"

Tina Walters raised her hand. "Because they're dangerous?"

"Yes," Abby said. "But not exactly in the way you think."

"Because they're . . . active," Eva Alvarez tried. "It's not like P&E, when it's about protecting yourself. They're for going on the offensive."

"Yes, they are. But that's not why they are so controversial."

The class sat silent, transfixed, as Aunt Abby studied every student in turn. "Doesn't anyone want to guess why—"

"Because weapons make you lazy." Bex's voice sliced through the room. "Because if you need a gun, it's probably too late for you to actually be safe."

"That's right." Abby smiled. "They are among the last things we teach because they are among the very last things you need to know."

It seemed like too much responsibility for just a bunch of moving parts. I glanced quickly down at the pile on the table, reached to finger the pieces of cool metal, the heavy springs, while my aunt talked on from her place in the center of the room.

"They will not keep your covers. They cannot recruit and train an asset. Make no mistake about it, ladies and gentleman, in the field, the only weapon that will truly keep you safe is your mind, and that is where any decent operative puts her time and her faith. And so what I teach you today is not the skill of a true spy. It's the skill of a killer."

Everyone was watching Abby. But not me. I was watching Zach. He kept his gaze glued to his hands. They were clasped together, resting on the table, his knuckles completely white.

"What I teach you today," Abby went on, "I teach you in the hopes that you never, ever need to—"

"Oh my gosh!"

I heard Tina scream, but I didn't know why until she added, "Cammie!"

Everyone was looking at me.

"What?" I said, and only then did I notice the gun in my hands. Heavy and cold, fully assembled and pointed at the door.

I wondered for a second where it had come from—how someone could have slipped it into my hands without my knowing.

"How did you do that?" My aunt's voice was cold and scared. "Cammie, how did you—"

She reached for the gun, but my hands were on some kind of autopilot, moving independently of my mind. They slid a bolt, split a section of the rifle away from the body, rendering the weapon useless—but it still felt like a viper in my hands.

"Cammie," Zach said, moving off his stool and easing toward me, "put the rifle—"

Before he could finish, I dropped it, heard it smash onto the desk. But it was still too close. I was afraid of what it might do, so I jumped back. The stool crashed against the floor, and I stumbled, trying to keep my balance, pressing close against the wall.

"Cammie, how did you do that?" Abby asked, eyes wide.

It was all I could do to look at her. "I don't know."

Chapter Eight

My feet beat against the damp ground. My heart pounded in my throat, and my arms pumped, my blood burned. I could have sworn I felt the fire, breathed the smoke. The tombs were closing in on me. Except I wasn't in the tombs.

"Cammie!" Macey yelled through the narrow tunnel-like space, but I couldn't turn back.

"Cammie!" Aunt Abby's voice echoed through the halls, and I knew she was chasing me, but I kept running and running, until finally the tunnels ended and I found myself in the small cavelike space that Bex and I had seen when we'd returned to school last January. My ankle hurt and my side burned, but I found the ancient ladder and started to climb, higher and higher into the belly of the school, until the ladder gave way to a staircase, and the staircase led me to the hidden door behind Dr. Fibs's file cabinets in the basement labs.

I was out of the tombs. I was safe. But I kept running.

Classes must have let out, because the halls began to flood with girls. Everything was a blur of books and backpacks, washing around me over and over like the icy river, and I felt like I might drown. I held tightly to the railing in the Hall of History, looking down on the foyer below, trying to catch my breath. My hands were shaking, and they felt like they no longer belonged to me but were instead the property of the girl who had washed up on the convent's banks.

That girl.

What had that girl known? And done?

The back of my neck was wet with sweat. My hair was too short, my uniform too big. And the music was back again, too loud inside my head, pulsing, drowning out the sounds of my school, the yelling and laughing of the girls—everything but the voice that came as if from nowhere, saying, "Hello, Cammie."

Suddenly there was a hand on my shoulder. But it felt like someone else who was turning, grabbing the hand, and kicking at the leg closest to me. That girl was spinning, using gravity and momentum to push the two-hundred-pound man toward the railing.

My hands stopped shaking. My knuckles turned white. But I didn't even feel the throbbing of the throat that pulsed beneath my fingers, or hear the cries sweeping through the gathering crowd.

There was yelling. Shouting. Teachers pushed their way through the bodies, trying to get to me—to stop me. To break me out of whatever trance it was that held me, until . . .

"Cammie?"

I heard the word. I knew the voice. There was a pale hand reaching slowly toward my own.

"Cam," Liz said softly. "That's Dr. Steve. You remember Dr. Steve, don't you? He's from Blackthorne—Zach's school. You remember Blackthorne."

I did remember Blackthorne. Blackthorne made killers. Assassins. Blackthorne was where Mr. Solomon had almost died, so I squeezed harder.

But then Liz's hand touched mine. Her skin was warm against my fingers. "The trustees said that Zach could stay if he had a faculty adviser, so Dr. Steve came. It's okay, Cam. You know him, don't you?"

Only then did I see the look in Dr. Steve's eyes; did I feel the terror pulsing through the crowd.

I must have pulled him from the railing, placed him gently on the floor, but all I remember was the way my hands shook, as if resisting. My hands were not my own.

"Cameron!" Professor Buckingham was at Liz's side. "Cameron Morgan, what happened here?" She turned to Dr. Steve. "Dr. Steve, are you—"

"I'm fine," he choked out, his face as white as a sheet. He looked like he'd just seen a ghost. It took me a moment to realize that the ghost . . . was me.

"I'm sorry," I said. "I'm sorry," I said again.

And then I stepped back, and for probably the millionth time in my life, I ran away.

Chapter nine

Covert Operations Report

Summer Summary by Cameron Ann Morgan

On the fourth of June, Cameron Morgan, a junior
at the Gallagher Academy for Exceptional Young
Women, left the school via the passageway behind
the tapestry with the Gallagher family crest, which
hangs in the basement corridor.

On September 30, The Operative woke up in a
convent on the Austrian border, high in the Alps.
She had nothing but a threadbare top and pants. At
some point, The Operative had lost her shoes, her late
father's journal, and her memory.

And that is everything The Operative remembers
about her summer vacation.

I looked down at the page and tried to pinpoint the exact
moment when homework became more about questions than

answers. I'd never felt less like a Gallagher Girl in my life. Even in the library, sitting in one of my all-time favorite window seats with the heavy velvet curtains drawn around me, it still seemed like I was a long, long way from home.

My breath fogged on the glass, mimicking the windows of the convent, and it might have been easy to think I was still there had it not been for the voice on the other side of the curtains saying, "Yeah, well, I heard the trustees were really worried about letting her back in."

"I know," another girl said. "She missed a lot of school."

I froze. I didn't want to move or breathe or do anything that might make the girls stop talking—or, worse, realize that the person they were talking about was two feet away and listening to every word.

"No, not the school part," the first girl replied, her voice a conspiratorial whisper. "The memory-loss part. I mean, my mom graduated with one of the trustees, and according to her, that is a really big deal. You saw what she did today." I felt my heart speed up. My hands shook. "No one knows if Cammie Morgan can be trusted."

I listened to the girls walk away, then gathered my things and slipped out as quietly as I could. I certainly didn't tell them they were wrong. Probably because I was afraid they were right.

There are fourteen routes a person can take from the library to the suite where I've lived since my first day of seventh grade. I knew which one was fastest, which was busiest, which one had the most awesome views, and the route that was most likely to make a girl freeze to death in winter.

But that night I didn't settle for any of those. Instead, I went straight for the part of the mansion that no one but the teachers ever used. The halls were long and narrow and empty, nothing but faculty living quarters and the occasional bookcase to mark the way.

It was easy to feel like I was the only person in the mansion (which was totally what I was going for), right up until the point when I heard a voice say, "Cammie?"

Zach was there. Zach was there, wearing nothing but a towel.

Blood rushed to my cheeks.

"Oh, I'm sorry. I—"

"What are you doing here?"

And just that quickly, the *being there* part became far more embarrassing than the *towel* part, to tell you the truth, because something in the way he was looking at me told me that I had completely and totally failed in my attempt to hide.

I didn't know which was more frustrating—his penchant for showing up at utterly embarrassing moments in my life, or the looks he gave me when he did—as though he knew more, saw more, understood better than anyone else on earth, and right then I kind of hated him for it.

I especially hated that it was probably going to happen a lot more now that we actually lived under the same roof.

"Cammie." Zach took a step closer when I didn't say anything. "Were you looking for me?"

"No. Why would you think . . ."

"My room." He gestured to the end of the hall. I hadn't really thought about where he was staying. It made sense, I guess, that they would move the Gallagher Academy's first (and probably last) full-time male student into one of the empty faculty rooms. "Is that why you're here?"

"Uh . . . no," I said, wishing I could claim I was on some mission, that I had some perfectly logical reason for being there, but I came up with nothing.

Note to self #1: Looking cool is a lot easier when you *are* cool.

"Where's Bex?" I asked.

"I don't know." Did he sound shocked or defensive? I couldn't really tell.

"Oh."

Note to self #2: Acting like you don't care is a whole lot easier when you *don't* care.

The silence that came next was deafening. I was just starting to long for the whispers of the library and the stares of Sublevel Three when Zach did the one thing that could make the moment worse.

He lowered his voice, asking, "Hey, are you okay?"

Were people ever going to stop asking me that? I honestly wanted to know. But not as much as I wished I knew how to answer it.

"Today"—he went on—"that wasn't really you, you know."

Maybe it was the ache in my head or the thought of him and Bex together all summer (and after) . . . Maybe it was the conversation I'd overheard, or all the other things that people were no doubt saying in all the places I couldn't hear. But for some reason his words didn't make me calm.

They made me angry.

"Oh, and you'd know the real me, would you? Because I'm pretty sure I've never known the real you."

"Cam—"

"I mean, all this time I thought your parents were dead, Zach. I distinctly remember your telling me your parents were dead."

"No. You remember *assuming* my parents were dead and my not correcting you."

"But actually your mom is the woman who's been chasing me for over a year," I went on, as if he hadn't spoken at all. "Which explains how you always knew so much, doesn't it?" I gave him a hard look. "At least that explains something."

"What are you doing here, Gallagher Girl?" He moved closer. He smelled like shampoo, and his skin glistened in the dim light. "What brought you here, really?"

I wanted to lie to him, but I didn't dare. I was too certain he'd see through it, through me. But then salvation appeared in the form of a slightly balding man at the end of the hall.

"Dr. Steve," I said calmly. "I came to talk to Dr. Steve."

Casually, Zach glanced behind him to look at his teacher, and then he turned back to me.

"Well then, don't let me stop you." He brushed past me. His voice was a whisper when he said, "Believe it or not, Gallagher Girl, I'm all out of secrets."

It was all I could do not to turn and watch him walk away, to pretend like I didn't care—that whatever rift there was between us didn't hurt. Luckily, there wasn't time for any of that, not with Dr. Steve walking toward me, saying, "Hello, Cammie. Teenage rendezvous?" he asked, with a glance at Zach and a chuckle.

"No," I said. "I'm here to talk to you."

"Oh, very well, then. What can I do for you?"

Dr. Steve's throat was a deep, crimson red. You could actually see the shape of my fingers outlined in the coming bruise, and all I could do was stare at it.

"I did that?"

It took me a moment to realize I'd spoken aloud. It took a moment more to remind myself it wasn't a question. "I did that," I said, forcing myself not to turn and run away from Dr. Steve and the bruise around his neck. I made myself look at it. Think about it. I didn't want to hide anymore.

"Did you say something?"

"Nothing. I mean . . . I'm sorry, Dr. Steve. I'm so . . . Are you okay?"

"Oh, I'll be fine." He smiled. "I promise."

Aside from the ring of red that circled his throat, he looked exactly like he had the day he'd first arrived at the Gallagher Academy, just after winter break in the middle of my sophomore year. He'd seemed in every way the opposite of the boys that he'd brought with him, and knowing the truth about what Blackthorne is—or was—didn't change that. If anything, he seemed even more out of place.

If anything, I felt even more ashamed.

"I really am sorry." I heard my voice break.

"I know you are, Cammie." Dr. Steve reached out as if to pat my back, but then he seemed to think better of it. To tell you the truth, I couldn't blame him. Even I moved away, unwilling to get too close.

"You couldn't have hurt me, Cammie," he said, but that wasn't true, and I knew it. He already wore the truth around his neck.

"The mind is a vast, complex thing," he said. "Your *memory* is a complex thing. No matter what you went through last summer, you couldn't kill someone. Not in cold blood. It isn't in you."

I remembered the way my hands moved, as if independent from the rest of me. I didn't know what was in me anymore.

He raised an eyebrow, studying me. "You don't believe me?"

"If Liz hadn't stopped me . . ."

"You stopped yourself."

"No, I didn't," I countered.

"Cammie, since when can Liz overpower anyone?"

It probably seemed like a fair point—Liz is the shortest, lightest, and least coordinated of us all. But he didn't know how truly powerful a great big mind inside a really determined girl can be.

"What kind of doctor are you?" I asked.

"Psychiatry is my area of expertise. My training is a tad more . . . specialized than that, though."

I wondered if *specialized* meant *really good at turning teenage boys into government assassins.*

"I don't teach people how to kill, Cammie," he said, as if reading my mind. "No. The Blackthorne Institute had a tradition of recruiting very disturbed young men and teaching them very bad things. But that, as they say, is history. It is my job to help troubled boys grow into strong young men. Or at least Joe Solomon *said* he was leading the movement to make that Blackthorne's new mission. But Joe Solomon said a lot of things he didn't mean, didn't he?"

A darkness crossed his face, and I thought, *He doesn't know.* Sure, the fact that Mr. Solomon was really a triple agent and wasn't actually loyal to the Circle was a closely guarded secret, but until then, almost every adult I knew had been *in on* the secret. It felt so strange seeing a lie at work.

Dr. Steve sighed. "But I guess we'll never know what Joe Solomon was thinking, will we? I'm sure his betrayal must have been very hard on you."

"Yeah," I said, the memory fresh. I absolutely meant it when I told him, "It was."

I thought about Joe Solomon, about a time when he was alive and well, and the biggest problem in my life was whether or not a boy thought I was pretty.

"What's really bothering you, Cammie?"

"I don't remember the summer."

He gave me a kind smile. "I know. That must be very hard."

"My mom says I shouldn't try to remember. She says—"

"Your mother is a very smart woman."

"Can you help me?" I pleaded. "I need to remember where I went and what I did. I need to know."

Dr. Steve considered this, then said, "Do you know what pain is, Cammie? It's the body's physical response to imminent harm. It is the mind's way of telling us to move our hand off the stove or let go of the broken glass."

"Will you help me?"

"The human mind is a miraculous thing. It is designed to keep us safe. Maybe your amnesia is your mind's way of saying that those memories could be harmful to you."

He was right, of course. My mother and aunt had said almost exactly the same thing. But there's a difference between knowing something in your mind and knowing it in your gut.

Through a window at the end of the hall, I saw the moon breaking through a cloudy sky. "It's been almost a year since the best spies in the world told me it might never be safe for me to leave this mansion."

"I know," Dr. Steve said softly.

I could still feel the rifle in my hands, the pressure of my fingers around Dr. Steve's throat, and so I told him, "Now I think it might not be safe for me to stay."

There's a power that comes with silence. I had grown to fear the unsaid thing. So it felt like a release to say it—to admit that the risk wasn't just inside our walls—it was inside my skin. I was willing to claw, scratch, and bleed until I'd found it.

"Your mother is correct, Cammie. You shouldn't try to force those memories." I opened my mouth to object, but Dr. Steve stopped me with a wave. "*However*, people who have sustained trauma often find it useful to have someone to . . . talk to. I'll speak with her, and if she agrees, then you can come see me Saturday afternoon. I'll be happy to help."

He smiled and swallowed, the red line on his neck moving up and down. "We'll see what we can do."

I wasn't exactly proud as I crept into the suite at one a.m., because, well, first of all, there was the creeping. And the fact that I actually stubbed my toe on the corner of my bed. But the hardest thing was realizing that I was no longer at home in my own room.

My things were unpacked and neatly folded, while my roommates' stuff was strewn around—the room a study in organized chaos like it always was in the middle of the semester. And all I could do was stand there wondering if I was destined to spend the rest of my senior year a half step behind.

"I see you." Macey sat up in bed. The light from the full moon fell through the window. Her eyes looked especially big and blue.

"Sorry," I whispered. "I didn't know anyone was awake."

"I know you didn't," Macey said. "That's why you decided it was safe to come in."

I sank onto my bed, but it felt strange—too soft compared to the cot at the convent. "I'm sorry, Macey," I said. "I don't know how many times I can say it. I'm sorry."

"Sorry you left or sorry you got hurt?"

"Both," I said. "And I'm sorry everyone is mad."

"You don't get it, do you?" Macey threw her covers off and stepped barefoot across the floor. "We're not mad because you left." She practically spat the words. I wondered if Liz or Bex might wake up, but neither stirred. "We're mad because you didn't take us with you."

I wanted to tell her that I'd do it all differently if I could. But that wasn't true, I realized. They were still alive, and that was what I'd wanted most of all. So I just looked down at my hands and admitted, "No one seems happy I'm back."

"You are back, Cam." Macey went into the bathroom and started to close the door. "Which means for the first time since you left, it's okay for us to be mad at you for leaving."

Chapter ten

Most teenage girls look forward to the weekend. Even at the Gallagher Academy, that is universally true. After all, who are we to deny the awesomeness of free-lab days and all-campus sparring competitions—not to mention the waffle bar and Tina Walters's legendary movie nights? But that weekend was something of an exception.

For starters, there's nothing like missing over a month of school . . . AT SPY SCHOOL! . . . to put a girl behind academically. Also, you don't really realize how much weekend time is actually hang-out-with-your-friends time until the aforementioned friends are acting all weird around you.

But that Saturday after lunch I didn't want to think about any of those things as I made my way to a closed door that, always before, had led to an empty office. The support staff had used it to store broken chairs and unused desks, but when I knocked, the door swung open and I could see the room had been completely transformed.

There was a tidy desk and an old wooden swivel chair like Grandpa Morgan kept in his office on the ranch. I saw a long leather couch and a cushy armchair beside a roaring fire. I hadn't realized how cold the rest of the mansion was until I stepped closer and lowered myself into the chair.

There were no diplomas or pictures, nothing personal at all, and I wondered if that was a Dr. Steve thing or just a shrink thing. Or maybe a Blackthorne thing. But the room was cozy and peaceful nonetheless, so I closed my eyes and felt the warmth of the fire washing over me.

"Cammie."

I heard the words but didn't want to open my eyes.

"Cammie, it's time to begin."

Then I started, bolting upright.

"I'm sorry. I . . ."

"You fell asleep, Cammie," Dr. Steve said, taking his place at the end of the leather sofa. "Are you having trouble sleeping in general?" he asked, but didn't really wait for an answer. "Do you wake up tired? Is your sleep fitful, erratic?"

"Yes," I said, realizing it all was true.

"I'm not surprised," Dr. Steve said, reaching for his glasses. "That's quite normal, you know."

"I think I would sleep better if I knew if my memory would ever come back—if it *can* come back. Can you tell me that much?"

Dr. Steve put his index fingers together, making an upside-down V against his lips. He seemed to weigh his options carefully before admitting, "I don't know."

"Then can you make me not dangerous?" I asked.

"Well, as I've already said, we don't know that you *are* dangerous. I need you to understand that you're not here to remember, Cammie. Your mother and I agree that it is important for you to talk about last summer—for you to come to terms with all that's happened." He took a deep breath and leaned slightly closer. "Can you do that? Can you wait? Can you work? Can you trust?" He sounded like he didn't know I was a Gallagher Girl. But then I realized I wasn't exactly *acting* like a Gallagher Girl.

So I nodded and said, "Yes. I'll do anything. How do we begin?" I asked, standing. "Should I lie down or . . ."

"Do whatever makes you feel comfortable. We're just going to talk for a while." He leaned back on the couch and crossed his legs. The fire crackled. There was a window to my left, and I found myself staring out at the kind of fall day where the wind is cold but the sun is bright. The sky was so clear and blue it might as well have been late June. But the leaves on the trees were turning, and the forest was laid out before me like a patchwork quilt.

"What's on your mind, Cammie?"

"It's supposed to be green," I said softly, as if speaking to the glass. "I keep thinking that it's the start of summer. It *feels* like the start of summer."

"I'm sure that's very confusing." Dr. Steve sounded sympathetic enough, but the problem wasn't that I was at risk of forgetting my jacket or not being prepared for Halloween.

Outside, girls were lounging on blankets by the lake; people ran laps around the woods, enjoying the sun while it lasted. And that was when I saw them, Bex and Zach leaving the P&E barn, both drenched in sweat, passing a bottle of water between them. And a part of me couldn't help but notice that they made a very striking couple (no pun intended).

"I think Bex and Zach are . . . together."

Okay, just to summarize, I had amnesia, a concussion, a knot on my head the size of a golf ball, half a semester's worth of work to make up, senior pictures to take, *and* an international terrorist organization that may or may not have still been after me at that moment. And yet, all I could say was, "He spent the summer with her family because . . . well . . . I guess he probably didn't have any place to go. He spent the summer with her," I said again, more for my benefit than Dr. Steve's.

"I know," Dr. Steve said. "I was a part of that decision."

"You were?"

"Do you think that was a mistake?" Dr. Steve asked.

"No." I shook my head and remembered that I had been the one to run away from home. But Zach . . . Zach didn't have a home to run to. Or from. "I'm glad he had someplace to go. It's just . . . he spent all summer with her family." Outside, Bex was sitting on Zach's ankles while he did sit-ups. With his shirt off. I felt my heart sink.

"I think I lost him," I said, and just then I realized that wasn't the half of it. "And her. I think I've lost them." Then I felt exhausted and turned from the window. I sank down into the chair and admitted, "But I guess they lost me first."

"And how do you feel about that?" Dr. Steve asked.

"Like maybe I had it coming."

"Do you think your friends are punishing you?"

"I ran away. I did something . . . stupid."

"Was it stupid?" Dr. Steve asked. It was the first time anyone—especially an adult—had said anything of the sort. "You must not have thought so at the time."

"No," I said, tugging at the memory. "It wasn't stupid. I was just . . . desperate. He said it first, you know—about leaving. About going away to try to find answers. Zach said it first."

"But you didn't take him with you," Dr. Steve said, and I shook my head.

"I didn't want anyone to get hurt."

"And yet *you* got hurt."

I didn't have anything to say to that. I leaned back in my chair. I wanted to close my eyes and curl up into a ball, sleep until my memory returned, but I knew that wasn't an option.

"That's a pretty tune," Dr. Steve told me, and I bolted upright.

"What?" I asked.

"That song you were humming. I like it."

"I wasn't humming," I said, but Dr. Steve looked at me as if I were crazy (a fact made far scarier because it might very well have been his professional opinion).

Then he shook his head and said, "I guess not. That must have been my mistake." He closed a notebook I didn't even realize he'd picked up, screwed the cap on to a really nice pen, and placed it in his pocket, then rose from the leather couch. "Very well. I think that's enough for today. It's getting late."

"No, it's not," I said, turning to the window, but the bright sky was dimmer. Dusk had come and I hadn't even known it.

"This time of year the days start getting much shorter, Cammie. I imagine—like the trees—that's something that would sneak up on you. And you slept for a long time."

"Oh," I said, standing. "Right."

"It will get better, Cammie," Dr. Steve said, stopping me in the door. "You'll get some rest and some space, and eventually it *will* get better."

Chapter ELEVEN

I don't know if it was all that talking, or the studying, or maybe the crash course that Courtney Bauer agreed to put me through in the P&E barn, but that night, going to sleep totally wasn't a problem. I mean, I'm fairly sure I managed to put on pajamas and brush my teeth, but I don't even remember my head hitting the pillow before I was one hundred percent out of it.

And dreaming.

There are a lot of kinds of dreams. Liz and her books about the brain have told me that much is true. There are "it's finals week and I just remembered a class I haven't been to all semester" dreams. Then there are "my friends and I are the stars of a popular sitcom" dreams. And, of course, there are the perfect day, perfect moment, perfect life dreams that come sometimes and make a person hit the snooze button for hours, trying to go back to sleep and make the perfect moments last.

This wasn't like that.

At first, it felt like the school must have been on fire, because the smell of smoke was so thick and real. I was too hot, smothered. Everything was crashing down around me, pushing in from all sides, and yet my arms couldn't move. I struggled against the bonds, heard talking and laughter, and fought harder.

I had to escape—outrun whatever it was that was chasing me—before the fire of the tombs caught up to me, before the smoke became too strong.

And then the fire was over. I was suddenly cold, and my feet were bare. My blood felt warm as it ran over my skin, but I kept running anyway.

I *had* to keep running.

There was something rough against my hands, and yet I kept clawing, fighting, trying to find my way out.

"I should have known you'd be here."

The words were new. They didn't belong there. And because of them I had to stop. To think.

"The least you can do is look at me when I'm talking to you."

And that was when I knew the dream was over. I turned to see Bex twenty feet away, arms crossed, staring daggers.

"Where am I?" I asked, but Bex just rolled her eyes.

"Yeah, *you're* lost. You know every inch of this mansion, Cam. If you expect me to believe that you of all people are lost—"

"This is the basement," I said, looking up and down the darkened hallway. I knew there was a narrow staircase behind

Bex, leading to the foyer above. To my left I saw the old Gallagher family tapestry. Behind it lay my favorite secret passage, and beyond that, the world.

"What am I doing here, Bex?" I asked, suddenly afraid. "What time is it? How did I get here?!"

But Bex didn't answer. She just looked down at my bare feet and said, "If you're running away again, you might want to remember your shoes."

She was starting to walk away when I yelled, "I'm not leaving!"

And then she spun back to me. The cold indifference was gone, replaced by a terrible rage as she shouted, "Then what are you doing wandering the halls in the middle of the night? What are you doing down here? Why . . . You know what? Never mind."

"I don't know. I was asleep and—"

"Sleepwalking?" Bex asked, then gave a short laugh. "Likely bloody story."

"I wouldn't lie to you, Bex," I heard myself shouting. "I have never lied to you."

For a second, her expression changed. My friend was there, and she believed me. She missed me. She was as terrified as I was. But whatever she was going to say next was drowned out by the sound of pounding feet.

"Cammie!" Abby appeared at the end of the hallway. "Rachel, I have her," my aunt yelled, but she didn't stop moving until she held me.

"Don't do that," Abby said, grabbing my shoulders and

shaking me. It was the first time anyone had dared to touch me since I'd tried to kill Dr. Steve. "Cammie, don't leave your suite in the middle of the night again. Do. Not. Do. That."

And then my mother was there, pushing past Bex, pulling me from my aunt's arms and into her own. "Cammie, sweetheart, look at me. Are you okay?"

"Of course she's okay," Bex said.

"Bex," Abby warned.

"She's fine! She's just a . . ." Bex started, but she stopped when she saw my mother's eyes.

"Cam"—Mom gripped my arms so tightly it almost hurt— "what are you doing here?"

At the end of the hall, Professor Buckingham and Madame Dabney were rushing closer, both of them in housecoats, their hair in curlers. It might have been funny. I might have wondered if the two of them had been in the middle of a sleepover, complete with mani-pedis and facials, if Liz and Macey hadn't arrived by then too. I saw Liz shaking, trembling in a way that probably had nothing to do with the drafty hall.

"I came here," I said, and I instantly knew it was true. "I came here last spring." I felt myself pointing to the tapestry and the passageway that lay behind it. "That was where I left."

"Impossible." Buckingham pulled her robe tighter. "That corridor was closed last December. I oversaw the work myself."

"There's a branch no one knew about. You missed it," I said, but my gaze never left my mother. "I remember coming here. . . . I came here and then . . ."

"What happened next, Cammie?" Liz asked, inching forward.

"I don't know."

"Yes you do," Liz said. "You know. You just have to—"

"Liz," Aunt Abby warned. "It's okay. She doesn't have to remember."

"Yes I do!" I yelled, but my voice faded, frustration replaced by fear as I faced my mother. "I know you don't want me to remember. I know you think I can't take knowing what happened to me. But don't you see? There's nothing worse than *not knowing*."

"Cammie," my mom started. "You're home now. It doesn't matter," she said, but I pulled away.

"It matters to me!" The hallway was too quiet for so many people. "You say I don't want to remember—that it's best not to know. Well, this"—I held up the raw, bloody fingers that, moments before, I'd been using to try to claw through the walls—"this is what not knowing is doing to me." My hand began to shake, and I couldn't stop myself. I yelled, "Why didn't you find me?"

There are so many things the Gallagher Academy trains us to do, but the most important, I think, is to watch. To listen. And when my mother looked at my aunt, I saw the faintest hint of something pass between them, a thread I had to follow and pull, even if it meant unraveling everything I'd ever known.

"What?" I asked, but Abby was shaking her head.

"It's nothing, Squirt."

"What?" I demanded, turning to my mother. "What aren't you telling me?"

"We did find you, Cammie." Mom looked down at the ground. She seemed worried and afraid and ashamed. "We were just a little too late."

Chapter twelve

Okay, to tell you the truth, I totally didn't know what was weirder—that someone knew *something* about my summer, or that, come Monday morning, I was crammed into a school van with my mother, my aunt, my new therapist, my roommates . . . and Zach.

I could hear him talking with Bex in the third row of the van, where the two of them sat next to Dr. Steve. I didn't look at them or speak. I kept my eyes glued to the road ahead. The only thing that broke my trance was when my mother would turn from the front passenger seat and glance back at me, almost involuntarily, as if to make sure that I was still there.

"Now, Zachary, how is that study schedule I designed for you?" Dr. Steve asked about an hour into the journey.

"Good," was Zach's reply.

"And your new courses . . . anything there I should know about?" Dr. Steve went on.

"Everything's fine," Zach said, but he didn't sound fine at all.

We drove through the countryside, along unfamiliar winding roads, and I didn't let myself think about the classes I was missing (six) or the number of tests that were being added to the ones I already had to make up (two). I wasn't at all concerned about the facts that my favorite jeans were now really big and my best friends were still pretty hostile. No, I didn't let myself think about that.

Instead, I watched the road and the landmarks, looked at every gas station and café as if *that* would be the sight that would spring the trap that was my memory and put everything back the way it was supposed to be.

And yet we kept driving in circles. Hours passed and we kept backtracking and stopping for no reason—all the standard vehicular antisurveillance techniques—until, after what seemed like forever, the van finally slowed and turned onto a narrow lane that was all but invisible in the dense forest, a path hidden beneath a thick layer of falling leaves.

Mom shifted in her seat and looked at me. "You know where we are?" she asked, and I nodded.

"It's coming back?" Liz said, her eyes bright. "See, I knew it would come back if we just had patience and faith, and now it's—"

"It's not back, Liz," Macey told her just as the van pulled out of the forest and into a large clearing. It was almost noon, and the sun glistened off a lake—its water as smooth as glass under the clear blue sky. Only the sounds of the birds that filled the woods broke the stillness. It was as if that place, too, were sleeping, waiting for its owner to wake up.

"It's Mr. Solomon's cabin," I said.

"Well, it's certainly . . ." Dr. Steve struggled for words. "Rustic."

Crawling out of the van, Liz held one hand up to shield her eyes from the sun, and I stepped out beside her. It felt good to stretch. Everything was cooler, fresher there. I waited for some memory to come rushing back and slap me across my senses—send the whole summer back in a blur—but nothing came.

All I felt was chilly air and warm sun and the sense that Summer Me was still hiding, lurking, like the shadows out there in those woods.

"I was here?" I said, turning to my mother and my aunt.

Dark sunglasses covered their eyes, and they didn't look like my family—they looked like agents who needed answers if they were ever going to see the other side of this particular mission.

Abby pushed her glasses onto the top of her head and studied me. "When we discovered you were gone, we notified all the key people, but we couldn't look for you like we normally would without alerting the Circle that you were missing. From an operational standpoint, that was the hardest part."

I didn't want to consider what the *mother* and *aunt* standpoints might have looked like.

"We had to keep it quiet," Mom went on. "We couldn't let them know you were in the wind. Alone."

I blinked, told myself it was the glare and not the words that were causing my eyes to water.

"But we knew how you were trained," Abby went on. "And we had an idea of what resources you had with you, and . . ."

"We knew you," Liz finished, smiling.

Bex sounded significantly less chipper when she pushed past me. "Or we thought we did."

Macey shrugged. "We didn't know where you were, Cammie," she said, stepping away from the van. "But this seemed as good a place as any to run."

It was, after all, where *she* had run. I smiled, knowing that at least I was in good company.

Walking toward the porch, I tried to search out something that was familiar, but I'd been to that cabin at least twice before. Once, after the Circle had made its first move—back when we'd thought the Circle was after Macey. And once again when Macey had run there on the eve of her father's big election. Those memories swirled together, and I didn't know where the old stopped and the new might have begun.

And there was something else, a worry or a fear tugging at the back of my mind.

"I don't think I would have come here." I stopped in the cabin's doorway and shook my head, as if even then it felt wrong to intrude. "I mean, how can you be *sure* I came here?"

Abby laughed. "Oh, you were good, Squirt." She walked to a cabinet and turned on a small TV. "But Joe was better."

A split second later, a blurry black-and-white picture filled the screen. It was divided into four quadrants, the images flashing, rotating from one camera to another, showing at least a dozen different angles of the cabin and the grounds.

"He had cameras," I said, unable to hide the awe in my voice.

Abby worked the remote control, and a moment later I was looking at a mirror into the past. My hair was long again, and even in black-and-white, I knew it was the brownish-blond color that had always seemed so boring to me, back before I realized that boring is seriously underrated.

Abby pushed a button, sending the surveillance footage into fast-forward while I stayed perfectly still, watching Summer Me sleeping and pacing. I did sit-ups and push-ups, and the sun rose and set. Rain fell and lightning flickered across the sky. Days passed and I stayed on that screen, alone.

"How long?" I asked.

"Four days," my mother said. "We think. We don't know exactly when you left, because . . ."

Her voice trailed off as Abby slowed the tape to regular speed. On the screen, the girl I'd been stood at the sink washing a plate and fork, staring out at the lake beyond the window, lost in thought. But then something must have caught her eye, because she turned and dragged a chair to the corner of the room and climbed onto it. My face filled the screen as I leaned close to the camera. Then the image dissolved into static, and the eight of us stood silent, no clue as to where Summer Me might have gone.

Abby put the remote down. "Judging from the time stamp

on the tape, that was two days before we came here looking for you. But by then, the cabin was empty. We didn't have any idea where you'd gone until the day you called from Austria."

I turned to see the plate in the drainer by the sink, sitting exactly where it was in the video. And then for the first time, it wasn't a question at all. "I was here."

No one said a word as I walked to the sink. "I don't feel anything," I said, reaching for the dish.

"It's okay, Cam," Liz told me. "Just . . . look."

Turning around in the room, I saw the narrow bed where I had woken after the attack in Boston—the first time the Circle had come for me. I recognized the small table from the video, ran my hands along the shelves of books.

"Why are you just telling me this now?" I asked, and felt something shift inside me. "Why didn't you bring me here first thing?"

"Cammie," Mom said, reaching for me.

"I need to remember," I told her. "I have to."

Mom looked as if that were the last thing in the world she wanted me to do, but she'd given up on fighting and didn't say a word.

"Why would you come here, Cam?" Abby asked.

"I don't know," I admitted.

"Not why *did* you," she clarified. "Why *would* you?"

It was just another test, a quiz, a hypothetical. I should know the answer. A Gallagher Girl with a big black spot in her head is still a Gallagher Girl.

I was still *me*.

"I didn't know for sure that I was going to leave until the night before I did it. I didn't have a lot of time to plan or pack. *Time*. I would have gone somewhere to buy time."

Mom nodded. "Yes."

"I couldn't get any supplies out of the sublevels without someone seeing or suspecting I was up to something, so I didn't have much I could take with me. I remember packing some clothes and"—I cut my eyes at Macey, whose wallet I had raided—"money. Sorry about that. I'll pay you back."

"Oh, I'll think of some way you can repay me," Macey told me.

"I needed a safe place off the radar and time to think and . . . gear. I needed gear."

Abby nodded. "Joe's storage shed was half empty when we got here."

"But mostly," I finished, as if she hadn't spoken at all, "what I really needed was time."

I felt as much as saw Zach looking at the room, his eyes following mine, but I could tell he was seeing a different story.

Mom must have noticed it too, because she asked him, "Zach, what is it?"

Zach's eyes slowly passed over the cabinets, the closet, and the bed. Then finally his gaze settled on the shelves of books.

"Those are out of order," he said, pushing the books aside to reveal a small section of paneling that was looser than the rest. A second later, he had it open and was staring into an empty hole in the wall.

"What was in there, Zach?" Abby said, pushing past him to

stare into the narrow opening in the paneling. "Was it weapons? Passports? Cash?"

"I don't know," Zach said, shaking his head. "He never showed me this."

"Think, Zach! What did Joe—"

"Not Joe." My mother stood perfectly still, her voice slicing through the crowded room. "That's not Joe's hiding place. It's Matthew's."

My father had been there—I could see it on my mother's face and feel it in my bones—not a memory, but an overwhelming sense of just knowing something, of feeling him, like a ghost inside the walls.

"I must have found it," I said, my voice flat and even. "I found whatever he left and then . . . I lost it." I looked at my mother, guilt and anger pounding through me. "I lost it. Just like I lost his journal and . . ." I didn't say *my memory*. I didn't have to.

"It's okay, Cam," Liz said, reaching for me.

But it wasn't okay. Not really. My mother kept staring at the empty compartment as if we'd missed something and a part of my father was still in there, calling to her through the years.

The screen door slammed, and a moment later Zach's voice came floating through the thin panes of the windows, saying, "I should have known she'd come here. I should have *known*."

"Don't blame yourself," Bex told him. "*You* aren't the one to blame."

And then I couldn't stop myself. I needed fresh air in my

lungs. I wanted to move, to feel my blood pumping, warming me. I longed to be free as my legs and arms worked independently from my mind.

I. Wanted. To. Run.

So I pushed open the door, darted around the corner of the cabin and started through the woods. Despite the throbbing of my ankle and the aching in my bones, it felt good to run. So I ran faster and faster until a twig snapped behind me, and I spun, my heart pounding hard in my chest.

"Sorry," Bex said. "I didn't mean to scare you."

"It's not an act, Bex," I said. "I really don't remember."

She crossed her arms and cocked a hip. "Why you left? Or why you didn't come back?"

"I *know* why I left," I shot back.

"Really?" Bex asked. "Because I don't."

"What was I supposed to do, Bex? Keep going until *you* ended up in a coma? Until Liz ended up dead?"

"You didn't have to go on your own," she countered.

"Yes! I did."

"CoveOps rule number twenty-one," Bex said. "'An operative should never enter a deep-cover situation without initiating emergency contact protocols.'"

"CoveOps rule number seven," I countered. "'The essence of Covert Operations is an operative's willingness and ability to work in deep cover operations *alone*.'"

Bex cringed. "Don't you quote Joe Solomon when he isn't here to tell you you're wrong."

"The fact that he isn't here just proves that I'm right!" I shouted, then lowered my voice. "You don't get it, Bex. Eventually, we all end up alone."

Bex glanced into the woods and back again. "In what scenario is *you on your own* preferable to *you with backup?*" I realized then that Bex might understand why I hadn't been a very good friend, but she'd never be able to forgive me for not being a very good spy.

And I couldn't help myself. I got angry.

"You know, I never got to ask how you spent your summer, Rebecca." Was invoking the power of her given name taking it a bit too far? Maybe. But I didn't care. "Do anything special?"

"You know . . . the usual. Swimming. TV. Scanning CIA bulletins for signs that my best friend was dead."

I spun and started walking through the trees, climbing to the top of the hill.

"Oh, I'm sure it wasn't all gloom and doom," I shouted over my shoulder to Bex, who followed behind. "Zach seems like quite the travel buddy. I mean, you did go to Budapest, right?"

"How did you know about—"

I stopped and wheeled on her. "I'm a spy, Rebecca." I saw my shadow on the ground, felt my too-short hair blowing around my face as I said, "So what was it? Mission with your parents? Vacation? Romantic getaway?"

"What do you *think* we were doing in Budapest?" Bex shouted. "Who do you think we were trying to find? If you have to ask, then you really don't know us at all."

And in that moment Bex didn't look like a girl who was after my boyfriend. She looked like a girl who had been terrified of losing her best friend. She and Zach weren't together—of course they weren't. They were just the people who most wanted to be with *me*.

Right then I realized that, to Bex, I was still gone.

"What do I have to do, Bex?" I yelled, following her down the other side of the hill and into a small clearing. "Tell me what I have to do or say or prove."

I stood shaking, my hands balled into fists as my best friend opened her mouth to speak but couldn't find the words.

She turned slowly and started to walk away.

"The Circle needs me alive!" I yelled, and watched her stop, but she didn't face me. "They would have killed you, Bex. They would have killed anyone but me without a second thought. But me . . . *they need me alive*."

"That's funny"—Bex turned—"because you look half dead from here."

And that was when the shot rang out.

Chapter Thirteen

My first thought was that I was wrong. In spite of everything—the sound of a rifle on that hillside seemed an almost ridiculous thing to hear. I told myself that the tree limb behind me had always been shattered. The loud noise was just a door slamming back at the cabin, the sharp crack carrying toward us on the wind.

It wasn't *really* a gunshot.

But then I was on the ground with Bex, sheltered behind a log, breathing in the rich, pungent smell of the decaying bark. Wet leaves clung to my skin. Toadstools sprouted from a knot in the log, and I knew it wasn't a dream.

It. Wasn't. A. Dream.

I wanted to scream or cry, but nothing came except the cold, certain knowledge that they'd found me. I'd run halfway around the world and lost all memory of the journey, but they'd found me.

"Cam," Bex said, her voice barely breaking through my mind. *"Cam!"* Her hand was on my arm, shaking me. Damp earth clung to her palms, and the dirt bit into my skin as she squeezed. "Cam, how far?"

"A hundred and fifty yards."

Had my mother heard the shot? I couldn't be sure. The trees were thick, and Bex and I had run farther than I'd thought, and we found ourselves on the other side of the ridge, the cabin and lake hidden from view by the rise of the hill behind us. We hadn't bothered with comms units. The tracking devices that Liz had spent hours perfecting last spring were all back at school.

When another shot rang out, piercing the trunk we lay behind, I knew that help may as well have been a million miles away.

"That was closer," I said.

Bex's eyes were wide as she nodded. "They're coming."

Sure, we had decent cover there, behind our log, but that wouldn't last for long.

"The Box Square method?" Bex suggested.

"The Brennan-Black technique?" I countered.

But neither option held any hope against a trained sniper with a clear line of sight, and we knew it.

"Stay here," I said, and started to my feet, but Bex was stronger—her reflexes even faster than I remembered—and I didn't have a chance to break free.

"Are you crazy?" she snapped, pulling me down.

"I'll circle around behind him. Or her. Or them. And then—"

"Are you *bloody crazy?*" she asked even louder, just as another shot rang out. I could see in her eyes that we were thinking the same thing: a hundred yards.

"Bex, let me go." I shook my head. "I can outflank them and come around from behind. I'll be fine. They won't—"

"Cammie, where was I standing?" Bex challenged even though I didn't think that was the time for a pop quiz. "*Where was I standing?*" Bex asked again, slower the second time. I looked at the place she'd been and did the mental math.

"He missed you by at least five feet, so let's figure he's moving to his left." I was right; I knew it. And yet there was something in Bex's eyes as I spoke. Somehow I knew she was a whole new kind of afraid.

"And that means..." I started, but I couldn't find the words. "And that means..." I tried again, but instead of the lessons of Joe Solomon, I heard the words I'd chanted to myself over and over for almost a year. *They need me alive. They need me alive. They need me alive.*

"Cam," Bex said, her voice low and steady, "it means they weren't shooting at me."

The birds had stopped their singing. The woods were quiet and still. And that was when I heard the music again. I squeezed my hands over my ears, but the sound grew louder and louder, and my heart rate slowed. The sun must have come out from behind a cloud, because everything seemed brighter. Clearer.

"Cammie." Bex was shaking me. Her eyes were wide with

terror. And I knew that we were in something of a clearing. Aside from the log, there was no cover for ten yards in any direction. We weren't sitting ducks yet, but the shooter was up and moving, and it was just a matter of time before he gained a line of sight.

We had to move from that position, and fast.

"Bex," I said, reaching for my best friend's hands.

"Yeah?"

Another shot rang out.

Seventy-five yards.

"I'm sorry." And before she could register the words, I kicked and sent my best friend tumbling, falling end over end, down the hill.

A split second later, I followed.

True, falling headfirst down a really big hill while you're still semi-concussed is probably not recommended, but I didn't have many other options at the moment. I landed with a thud against a large mound of blackberry bushes. Thorns sliced into my skin. My head swirled and throbbed, and I thought I would be sick. But there was a shadow overhead, and I knew that my plan (if you want to call it that) had worked, and we'd made it out of the clearing and into the cover of the trees.

Bex had landed twenty feet away from me. Good, I thought. Stay there. Stay safe, away from me.

But it was too late. She was already up and moving toward me, like a cat.

"How many?" Bex said, her breath even and steady. A piece

of moss clung to her hair, and mud stained her cheek, but she didn't move to wipe any of it away.

"Just one," I said, then considered. "I think."

I hoped.

I saw a figure moving through the trees behind us, up the hill. He wasn't big, necessarily, but he was agile and quick and lean.

And closer. Coming so much closer.

But there were no more gunshots, so either he was making up too much ground to fire, or else our move had worked, and he had lost sight of us.

We were deep in the middle of three hundred acres of timber and rocks and falling leaves. The main gravel road was probably two hundred yards down the hill. Now that we'd reached the cover of the trees, we could go down to the county road and hopefully circle around to the cabin from below. Or we could swing around wide and climb up the hill, try to pass the sniper, and make it over the rise.

"High ground?" Bex asked, reading my mind.

"High ground," I agreed, and together we started to run.

You might think in these situations the advantage lies with the grown man with the high-powered rifle, and not with the two teenage girls in training.

Well, that, of course, depends upon the girls.

Bex was ahead of me, running up the hill, jumping over limbs and landing on rocks. Weightless. Effortless.

I, on the other hand, had an ankle that was still semi-sprained and a set of lungs that were far from operating at full capacity, and I didn't know which was scarier: the sniper on our trail or the thought of Bex knowing that I'd lost my stamina *and* my memory over my summer vacation.

We could hear breaking twigs and panting breaths. Bex and I skidded to a stop, pressed ourselves against a couple of trees, and I called upon every ounce of chameleon in my blood.

The sun was high overhead—a little after noon—and the light broke through the canopy of the trees. It looked like a kaleidoscope across the ground, but Bex and I were shrouded in shadow, and I tried to remind myself that being invisible isn't about camouflage and cover as much as it is about stillness and calm. I leaned against the tree and willed my body to be just an extension of the bark. In my jeans and dark sweatshirt, at that angle and in that light, the assassin could have looked right at me and not seen me, as long as I was still enough. But staying still wouldn't save us, and I knew it.

"Bex," I whispered. "I'm holding you back."

"Don't be silly. Of course you aren't."

"Of course I *am*. He's a lone gunman, and we have numbers."

She must have read my mind, because she snapped, "We're not splitting up, so you can bloody well forget—"

"What would Mr. Solomon say?"

"I'm not leaving you," she said, totally sidestepping the question.

"You're not leaving me, Bex." I smiled. "You're doubling our chances."

Just then a shot rang out and pierced a tree ten feet behind us. The time for arguing had officially run out. I could see it in my roommate's eyes as she looked at me.

"I'll see you at the cabin," she said. It was a warning.

"I'll see you at the cabin," I said, and like that, she was gone.

It wasn't scary, being alone. Bex was safer the farther she was from me. And me . . . well, I'd pretty much forgotten what safe felt like anyway. So I leaned against the tree, trying to catch my breath. The top of the ridge was probably eighty yards uphill over rough terrain.

I could do it, I told myself. I had to do it. Bex was going to be waiting for me at the cabin.

And that's when the breeze picked up and the light flickered, shining for one second off a thin wire that ran between two of the trees in Joe Solomon's forest.

Wait. I stopped and thought. *Joe. Solomon's. Forest.*

The thin wire lay across a narrow path, almost obscured by fallen leaves. And if I knew Mr. Solomon, then I could have sworn that the wire was designed to trigger something—tell someone—that something was wrong on that hillside.

So I didn't let myself think about it anymore—not about how little cover there was between my position and the narrow opening of the path. I didn't calculate how long it would take my aunt and mother to reach me, or the odds that I was wrong and tripping that wire would do nothing at all.

I just turned my brain off and ran into the small open area, and when I reached the wire, I bolted through it, felt it brush against my ankle and break, and I didn't slow down until I heard the shot fire and felt my body crash against the ground, warm blood spreading over my skin.

Chapter fourteen

There was a crack as a second shot pierced the air, and a bullet hit the tree exactly where I'd been moments before. And yet I didn't move. Couldn't move. Someone lay across me, pressing down. And when Dr. Steve said, "Cammie, someone's shooting. . . ." I didn't think I'd ever heard anyone more afraid.

"Dr. Steve, what are you doing here?"

I wanted him to say that the others had heard the shots and come looking for us—that help was on the way. But instead he shook his head. "When you left the cabin, you seemed so upset. I thought you might want to . . . talk."

I didn't want to talk. Talking felt like the most useless thing in the world.

"Cammie, I . . ."

I'd never realized how pale Dr. Steve's skin was until it stood in contrast to the red blood that was oozing down his arm.

"You're hit," I said.

"It's just a . . ." He trailed off, grimacing in pain. "Scratch."

I pushed him off of me and examined the wound. He was right. It wasn't much more than a scratch—a through-and-through—but Dr. Steve wasn't like us. He wasn't trained for fieldwork, and he winced as if he might be sick. But I didn't have time for sick. There was a sniper in the woods with an excellent line on us, and our luck wouldn't hold out for long.

"Here," I said, dragging him around the tree and hopefully into better cover. "Put pressure on it."

I pulled off my hoodie and started to press it against the wound, but drops of blood were already falling, landing on the rocks at my feet.

Red drops on white stone.

It was a strangely beautiful sight. I couldn't pull my eyes away, and suddenly I felt dizzy. The world was spinning, pulling me backward through time and across space until everything grew incredibly slow—as if the whole thing had happened before, exactly like that. But different.

It was a different mountain. Different rocks. Different blood.

"I was bleeding," I said as the memory I couldn't quite name came rushing back. The wind felt colder, the air thinner. Was that a gunshot or the sound of snow crashing through the trees? I wasn't sure of anything anymore.

"Cammie . . ." Dr. Steve said slowly, his lips a thin hard line.

"I was running. And bleeding. But it was finally light out. I could finally see the sky."

"Cammie, it's—"

"There was blood on the ground and on the trees," I said

numbly, recalling how I hadn't bothered to hide my tracks. "They were getting closer. But I was so weak. I was just so weak . . . I wasn't going to get away. I shouldn't have gotten away."

The memory was stronger then, deeper. It was like I was there—really there—and everything was the same, the wind and the smells and the red, red blood. Everything was exactly the same except the screaming.

No, the screaming belonged on a different mountain. I shook my head and focused on the sound of Bex's cries. I wasn't in Austria. And I wasn't broken or beaten or worn. Not anymore.

I wasn't going to be weak anymore.

"Cammie!" Dr. Steve yelled, genuine panic filling his eyes. "Don't!" He tried to reach for me, pull me back to the relative safety of the ground; but even with two good arms, there was no way Dr. Steve could have stopped me.

I no longer felt my ankle. Adrenaline pounded in my veins. I ran faster, leaping over fallen logs, skirting around trees and rocks. My arms pumped at my sides as I pushed my way through the thick underbrush and dense pines. Faster and faster I ran until, finally, I could make out my best friend's shape on the horizon.

She was on an outcropping of rock near the top of the hill, the shooter maybe three feet away. Bex lunged, striking the man, but he didn't fall. And as he shifted his weight, Bex crashed to the ground.

"No!" I screamed just as the man raised the butt of his rifle.

But Bex twisted and kicked, sending the gun out of his hands and skidding across the rocks.

And I kept running.

Bex swept her leg and knocked him off his feet. But the man was so fast, it didn't matter. He hit Bex hard across the face, sending her tumbling down the hill.

Everything seemed to happen in slow motion as I reached the top of the ridge. There were no trees or shadows, and that was probably why it was so easy to see the knife—shiny and clean. The sun glistened off the blade as the gunman pulled it from a sheath on his leg and lunged toward Bex.

She tried to block the blow, but the man was so strong. And the next thing I knew, there was a splatter of blood and Bex was screaming, her face a mix of shock and fear and . . . relief as the man fell to the ground and didn't move again.

The gun was in my hands.

My finger was on the trigger.

The sights were still trained on the man—on the red mass spreading out from his chest, covering the place where his heart should have been. He lay so still, as if he might be resting, the knife still glistening—shiny and clean—in his outstretched hand.

"Cammie!" It was Liz's voice. "Cammie, Bex . . . Cammie!" she yelled. I heard her running up the hill, and then she came to a sudden stop. "Oh my gosh," she said, staring at the body at Bex's feet. I heard her begin to gag and vomit, but I didn't look away from the man who lay lifeless on the ground.

There was a weight on the rifle, a tug, but I held it steady, kept the assassin in my sights.

"Cammie," Zach said, pulling harder on the barrel. I didn't know where he'd come from or how long he'd been there, but his voice was in my ear, sounding worried and afraid. "Cammie, give me the gun."

"Give it to him." Abby and my mother were running along the ridge toward us. Abby yelled, "Now!"

And only then did I feel like it was okay to let the rifle— and my defenses—fall.

Abby walked to the body and called to my mother. "Rachel, any others?"

"No. I think he's alone."

"Well, he might not be alone for long." Abby took the gun from Zach and yelled, "Everyone, get to the van."

"Cam?" My mother was looking at me. "Cammie, sweetheart, are you hurt?"

I wasn't hurt. I was numb. And I liked it.

Mom shook my shoulders. "Cammie, you need to—"

"Rachel," Abby snapped, cutting her off. "We have to go. Now."

Bex walked to the body and started digging through the gunman's pockets.

"He's clean, Bex," Zach told her. "He wouldn't make the mistake of coming here with anything he couldn't be found with. He was too good for that."

"I've got to check—"

"He's clean." Zach shook his head and turned to Liz, put his arm around her, and started up the hill. "Liz, we have to go."

"Cammie killed him," she said, the color gone from her already pale face.

"He's not a good man, Liz," Zach said, turning her around. He made her stare into his eyes. "He is not a good man. It's good that he's dead."

"It's good," Liz repeated.

"I don't know who he is," Zach told her. "I don't know why he's here, but I know Abby's right. We have to go."

"We know something." My voice was frail, as if it were just a shadow who was speaking.

Liz looked at me. "What?"

"We know they don't need me alive anymore."

Chapter fifteen

What I said to my mom: *I'm fine.*

What I said to my aunt: *It's okay.*

What I said to the doctor: *It doesn't hurt.*

But I wasn't fine. It wasn't okay. And it did hurt. Everywhere. Even in the darkness of the suite, hours later, I could feel my roommates watching me. So I closed the bathroom door and turned the shower on high, the pounding of the water drowning out the pounding of my thoughts as I gripped the sink and leaned closer to the girl in the mirror.

Dirt and mud clung to her skin. The bruise at her hairline was a sickly shade of purple and green. It looked like the kind of thing you might find floating on a pond at the end of summer.

The only light came from the night-light Liz had plugged into the outlet by the sink on the first day of seventh grade, and yet it was easy to see the mud and grime. My hoodie was gone, somewhere—covered with Dr. Steve's blood. New bruises blended with old, up and down my arms. The mirror began to

106

fog, closing in on me like I was about to lose consciousness, but I had to stay awake.

"Cammie." It was Liz's voice, her familiar, faint knock on the bathroom door. "Cam . . ."

"I'm fine," I said, for what felt like the billionth time. "I'm . . ." And then the words didn't come.

I'm not fine.

I looked at the girl in the mirror, staring back, broken and bruised.

I'm not her.

The thought shook me.

I'm not her! I wanted to scream, but it was like I'd lost my voice as well as my memory.

That girl had come back from summer break. She had taken things from me. Zach and Bex. My summer. My life.

I had left, but that girl was the one who had come home.

And that girl was different.

I looked down at my hands. They were sore and red and stained with Dr. Steve's blood.

That girl had blood on her hands.

Her hands knew things I wasn't supposed to know. She did things I didn't want to do.

I hated that girl, hated her as much as I hated the Circle. Distrusted her more than I distrusted Zach's mom. Enemies are nothing compared to traitors, after all. It's the people you hold closest who have the most power to make you bleed. And that girl . . . she was as close as anyone could possibly be.

I didn't mean to do it, but in the next second, a hair dryer was flying through the air. It hit the mirror, and I watched the girl shatter; but she was still there. I could see her. So I grabbed Macey's curling iron and hurled it at the image, and another piece of mirror cracked and crashed; but the noise was nothing compared to the banging on the bathroom door.

"Cammie, open this door!" Macey yelled. "Open this—"

"Cam!" Bex yelled, and a split second later the doorjamb splintered and Bex was rushing toward me, yelling, "Cammie!" She took one look at the shattered glass and the look on my face and said, "Cam, are you okay?"

But I didn't answer. I was pulling open drawers and scavenging inside, saying, "I hate her. I hate her."

I looked crazy. I was acting crazy. But I knew exactly what I was doing when I picked up the scissors.

"Cam!" Liz yelled.

But I just reached for the black hair that didn't feel like my own, grabbed a handful, and . . .

"Cammie, no!" Bex snapped, like you might yell at a dog for chasing cars. It was a warning that I didn't want to hurt myself. "No," she said again, and with one motion, she twisted the scissors from my hand.

"I killed a man, Bex."

"He would have killed me," she said slowly, swagger gone. Ever since I'd known her, Bex had seemed practically bulletproof; but standing there, with blood on her sleeve, she trembled. "I would have died."

"I don't even remember picking up the gun," I said, realizing that that was the most terrifying thing of all.

108

"*I'm alive* because you picked it up," Bex told me.

I turned to the mirror and gently pulled the scissors from Bex's grasp. "*She* did that." I reached for a piece of hair and was just about to cut when Bex caught my hand again.

"Don't do that," she said, and for the first time in months, I saw Bex smile. "I seem to remember a bangs incident in the eighth grade that taught us you are *not* the person who should do that."

And then the strangest thing happened: my roommates laughed. I looked in the mirror and realized I was laughing too.

Macey turned to Liz. "Dr. Fibs has hydrogen peroxide in the lab, right?"

Liz sounded almost offended. "Of course he does."

"Get it," Macey said, turning back to me. "We have work to do."

It wasn't like we talked a lot. But then again, it's not like there was all that much left to say. We'd seen things. We'd done things. And I wasn't the only one who was still waiting for me to come home from my summer vacation.

I leaned over the sink and let Bex wash and bleach my hair. Then Macey took the scissors and trimmed away my dead, uneven ends. I sat, letting my best friends work around me, watching as the person I had been last summer washed away down the drain.

Chapter Sixteen

That night I couldn't sleep.

It might have been the adrenaline or the new scratches on my body. I told myself it had something to do with the smell of hydrogen peroxide which lingered in the air, but if that was it, then I was the only one it bothered. My friends were around me, snoring softly. Bex had an ice pack on her shoulder. Macey slept with a self-satisfied smirk across her face. And Liz was listening to headphones, memorizing the audio version of some ancient textbook while she dreamed.

But not me.

I lay on my back, staring at the ceiling, and every time I closed my eyes, I saw the blood on Dr. Steve's sleeve. Every time I almost drifted off to sleep, I heard the music, soft and lingering in the corners of my mind.

Finally, I threw the covers aside, crept into the bathroom with its busted mirror, and pulled on my uniform as quietly as I could.

"Where are you going?" Bex asked when I reappeared. She was sitting up in bed and squinting at me through the dark.

"Waffles," I told her. Bex raised one eyebrow, doubtful. The clock beside her bed read five forty-five a.m. "The kitchen will be open soon, and I want..." There were so many ways that sentence might have ended. Answers. My memory. But most of all I needed my mom to hug me and smooth my hair and tell me I wasn't a terrible person for pulling that trigger the day before.

So instead I just said, "Waffles. I'm craving waffles."

Bex rolled onto her side. "Tell your waffles hi for me."

There's something especially beautiful about the Gallagher Academy when the classrooms are dark and the halls are quiet. Moonlight falls through the stained glass windows; shadows creep across the stairs. It looks like the most peaceful place on earth. Too bad every spy knows that looks can be deceiving.

"Thank you for coming."

At the sound of Professor Buckingham's voice, I froze in the middle of the Hall of History, staring down at the foyer below.

"You really didn't have to rush," Buckingham said, closing the front door behind two women I'd occasionally seen but had never met.

They wore heavy coats and heavier expressions, and there was no uncertainty at all in the younger woman's voice when she said, "I assure you, we did."

"Where's Rachel?" the older woman asked.

"In her office."

"And the girl?" the young woman said.

Buckingham seemed to bristle a little at the word, but she folded her hands and said, "Sleeping." She gestured toward the Grand Staircase. "We'll be ready to begin soon." I slid around the corner while they climbed. It was easy for me to be invisible in the long shadowy corridor. I was still the Chameleon, after all, as I stood watching the trustees descend upon the Gallagher Academy.

Knowing they were there because of me.

There's a passageway I never use. Or, well, hardly ever. Seriously, that particular passageway is an EMERGENCY SITUATIONS ONLY kind of thing, and, call me crazy, but it was starting to feel more than a little emergency-ish by the second.

The trustees were there.

In five and a half years at the Gallagher Academy, I'd seen them at my school maybe a half dozen times (and that included the time Dr. Fibs accidentally activated—*but didn't detonate!*—a nuclear warhead in the labs). This wasn't a meeting, I knew. This was an emergency.

"Where are you going?"

I stopped and turned, and wondered if I'd ever get used to the sight of Zach in our halls, wearing his official Gallagher Academy workout gear—the clean white T-shirt with the official school crest. It was maybe the best cover legend I'd ever seen: Zachary Goode, preppy schoolboy. But I couldn't touch him. It was like there was still a fire between us. I wondered if we would ever leave the tombs.

"Cammie," he said, urgency rising in his voice, "are you—"

"I'm fine," I said, darting into a sitting room that nobody ever used. "Hold this." I picked up the fireplace poker and moved it out of the way.

"Gallagher Girl . . ." He sounded skeptical, but that didn't stop me from pressing against the Gallagher Academy crest that was engraved into the mantel. Zach stood in wonder as, one by one, the stones began to roll away.

"I just want to check on something." I ducked down and stepped over the ashes of a fire that had long since gone out, careful not to leave any tracks.

"Does this *something* have anything to do with the two limos that just pulled up outside?" Zach asked, and followed. But I didn't answer.

"I thought the passageways were all blocked off," he said from behind me.

"The ones they know about are closed up. And besides, this one doesn't go outside. It's not a perimeter threat."

The passageway was dim and tight. Old wooden beams cut through the space, covered with dust. There were spiderwebs and a mouse or two, and Zach had to crouch low and turn his broad shoulders at odd angles to follow, but he did. And he didn't say another word.

"Originally, a lot of these were servants' hallways." I leaned down and slipped under a beam. "For a while, during the Civil

War, the mansion was a stop on the Underground Railroad. It wasn't until Gilly took the building over and turned it into a school that she really started expanding everything, though. She had to keep up appearances, you know. It was just as important then that the truth about us stay a secret."

I went on, slipping forward as quiet as a ghost, toward the narrow passage that looked through a small opening, right into my mother's office.

Mom sat stoically behind her desk. Abby was at her right side, standing almost at attention. I felt Zach catch my arm. "You don't want to be here, Gallagher Girl."

"It's the trustees, Zach. The trustees never come unless something big is going on."

"If it were something that pertained to you, then you'd be in the room and not spying on it."

"Why are you up, Zach?" I asked, and I could tell the question had knocked him off his game.

He actually stumbled a little before saying, "At Blackthorne, we ran drills every day at dawn. Old habits die—"

"How did you find me?" I went on, too exhausted to listen to any more lies. "Mom told you to keep an eye out for me this morning, didn't she?"

"Cammie," Zach started.

"She didn't want to risk my seeing . . . this." I turned back to the small opening and studied the two trustees who sat at the center of the room. Professor Buckingham stood by the windows, and everyone seemed focused on the speakerphone that sat on the edge of my mother's desk.

114

"Rachel, I understand your concerns," a male voice boomed from the box.

"With all due respect, sir," Abby said, "I don't think you do."

"Abigail," the older of the trustees warned.

"We told you Cammie went to the cabin when she left here last summer," Abby said. "And now it looks like the Circle has probably had the place under surveillance since the day she got back."

"Agent Cameron, are you implying . . ."

"That the CIA has a leak, sir?" Abby guessed. "Yes, I am." She took a deep breath, and I got the impression that this was well-worn territory in a long conversation. "Where the Circle is concerned, the CIA always has leaks."

"That wouldn't be a concern if you'd just keep the girl *inside the school*," said another male and unfamiliar voice. I wished the Baxters were there. I got the impression that Mom and Abby needed all the allies they could muster.

"Truthfully," the younger trustee started, "given recent events, I'm far less concerned about whether or not it's safe for her to leave than whether or not it is safe for her to stay."

"Cammie is not dangerous," Mom said.

"Really, Rachel." The older trustee cocked an eyebrow. "I think there's a body in the morgue at Langley that says otherwise."

"That was self-defense," Buckingham snapped from her place near the window.

"Yes, it was." The older woman turned to her. "This time. But can anyone swear that there won't be a next time?"

115

No one said a thing. I guess none of them was certain of the answer. It took me a moment to realize: neither was I.

"If it's true that the Circle no longer needs—or wants—her alive, then the girl faces a serious threat, that's certain," the younger trustee said. "But what we would like to know is whether or not *she is* a threat."

I felt myself tremble. My hands balled into fists. For a second I thought I was seeing things, my vision going as black as my memories as the older trustee turned to my mother and asked, "*Is* the girl stable, Rachel?"

"The girl's name is Cammie," Aunt Abby said.

"Is she capable of betraying the confidence and security of this school?" the trustee went on. "Rachel, you had to know that your daughter wasn't . . . herself."

My mother didn't turn away from the accusation. She held her head high. "Oh, I know that very well."

How many times had my mother warned me not to pick at my memories, not to go digging around in the dark? I realized then that Mom and Abby weren't just afraid of what I might have lived through. They were terrified of what I might have done.

"When the Circle had her . . ." Abby started, but one of the trustees cut her off.

"*If* the Circle had her."

"What are you saying?" Mom countered.

"Maybe they never had her at all. Maybe they sent her back for some reason," the trustee said, running through the options.

"Cammie is no double agent. She wasn't turned," Abby snapped, but the trustee talked on.

"The truth is, we don't know anything. Your daughter ran away, Rachel," the younger trustee said. "I think I speak for everyone when I say we're very interested to know exactly who came back."

Chapter Seventeen

I didn't want to watch any more. I couldn't bear to listen. So I pulled away and pushed farther into the tunnels, deeper and deeper into the belly of the school. Zach was taller and stronger, but I had a body that was made to disappear, and I could hear him chasing after me, struggling to keep up.

Eventually, the tunnel widened. Pale, predawn light sliced through the room from a dusty, narrow window, and I stood, panting, the trustees' words echoing in my head.

"Don't do that." Zach grabbed my hand and spun me toward him. "Don't ever run away again."

"I killed someone," I said.

"You saved Bex," he countered.

"They think I'm dangerous. They think—"

"They don't know you!"

My hair was almost its normal color. My uniform didn't swallow me quite like it had a week before. Slowly, my body was starting to feel more like my own. But I wasn't the girl I'd been when I left, and I knew it. I shouldn't have been surprised that the best spies in the world would know it too.

"They don't know you," Zach said again. He grabbed my hands. "*I* know you."

"They're strangers," I told him.

"Yeah," he agreed, as if that should make me feel better.

"Impartial, informed, unbiased strangers." I pulled away and looked up into his eyes. "And they think something is wrong."

I wanted him to argue, to say that everything was going to be fine. It was a lie I was ready and willing to believe. But the words didn't come. Instead, Zach ran a hand through his hair and asked, "Why did you kill him, Cammie?"

"I don't know," I admitted. "I don't even remember doing it. I was—"

"Why didn't you let *me?*"

Okay, now's probably the time to say that I totally wasn't expecting that.

Zach leaned closer to me, covering the minuscule space in a step. "They teach us how to do those things. At Blackthorne."

It felt strange to have him volunteer anything about his school—his life. It felt even weirder to have him get things wrong.

"The Gallagher Academy doesn't exactly leave its graduates clueless on the subject, you know." I didn't mean to sound offended, but I was.

But Zach was shaking his head. "They teach you how to

save lives. They teach us how to *take them.* And then, how to live with ourselves after..." He touched the cool glass of the window. "It's all my fault."

"Nothing is your fault."

"I told you to run away." Zach shook his head. "I gave you the idea."

"No you didn't," I said. "I'd known for a long time that it was my best option."

"You should have taken me!" Zach didn't seem to realize he was shouting. And if he had known, I seriously doubt he would have cared. "You needed me."

He reached for the spot on my head, but I sidestepped his touch and moved away.

"Why? So I could watch Mr. Solomon's protégé throw himself on another bomb to protect me? So that I could watch someone else get hurt?"

"So we could keep each other safe."

"News flash, Zach. I am safe!"

He looked at me like I was a crazy person. Trust me. I'm a teenage amnesiac. It's a look I know pretty well.

"You could have died, Cammie."

"I'm breathing," I said, defiant. "And I'm home and—"

"You could have died," he said, easing closer.

"I'm fine," I said just as Zach reached me.

"You could have died," he said just as my tears finally came.

I kept shaking my head, saying over and over, "I don't remember. I don't remember."

Was I talking about my summer, or about picking up the gun? Pulling the trigger, or assembling the rifle on my first day back to school? I didn't know. Everything ran together in a blur.

"I killed someone."

"I know."

"I killed someone, and I don't even remember pulling the trigger. That can't be normal. You take a man's life, you should remember it. You should think about it. You should know what you're doing and . . ."

But I never finished because then Zach's lips found mine. His hands burned as they left my arms and moved through my hair, bracing the back of my neck. My head still hurt, but there was no music playing.

"I remember this." I felt my hand run along his chest, his breath warm on the side of my face. I breathed him in—Zach. "I remember this."

And then he kissed me again, and the kiss was all that mattered. He pulled back, traced his lips across the tender place on my head.

"I . . ." I heard my voice trail off, my thoughts centering on the single thing I really had to know. "Are you afraid of me, Zach?"

"No."

I looked at him, felt my hands shake and my voice break as I whispered, "I am."

Chapter Eighteen

You might think being the target of an international terrorist organization, an amnesiac, and a girl with hair dyed in the middle of the night by Macey McHenry would make people stare at you. Well, try walking into the Grand Hall with seriously puffy eyes while holding hands. With a boy.

"Well, how are *you* this morning?" Tina Walters said, and I knew she had no idea what had happened on our field trip, or who had come to our door before the sun had risen. Or why.

I hoped they would never know why.

"Scoot," Zach told her, and Tina smiled, sliding down to make room for the two of us on the bench.

He reached for the bacon in the center of the table, handed the plate to me.

"No thank you," I said. "I'm not hungry."

"I thought you wanted waffles," Bex said, eyeing me.

"I—"

"Here." Zach dropped a waffle onto my plate and reached for the butter.

"No, I'm really not—"

"You're too skinny," said Liz, a girl who I swear once bought a pair of pants that were a size double zero and had to have them taken in.

"It's true," Macey added. "Some girls look better with some fullness in their face."

So I buttered my waffle and took a piece of bacon from the plate.

Bex smiled at me from across the table. "The hair looks good." She turned to Macey. "Good call on the trim."

"Yeah," Macey said, eyeing her handiwork. "It's a patch job, but it's better."

Everything looked normal. Everything sounded normal. But I still had cobwebs on my sweater and dust on my skirt, and the words I'd heard were still there, rattling around inside my head so loudly I thought that I might scream.

Zach must have sensed it, because he moved his hand to the small of my back and rested it there.

"Did you see your mom?" Bex reached for the carafe and poured herself a cup of hot tea as if nothing were wrong; but all I could think about was what I'd heard her say on my first night back: *They're pretending.*

I didn't say what I was thinking—that I was pretending too.

"Um . . ." I mumbled, stumbling over the answer. "She was busy."

Everyone nodded. No one thought to ask, *Busy with what?*

So I ate my waffle and drank my juice and didn't say a word about what Zach and I had overheard in my mother's office.

"I'm stuffed," I said ten minutes later, and nobody argued as I stood and started for the door.

With my friends and Zach around me, it might have been easy to pretend that we were typical students starting a typical day. But then Liz dropped her backpack.

Trust me when I say it was a sight I'd totally seen before. The floor was littered with textbooks and note cards, piles of paper and an extensive collection of highlighters that Liz herself had patented. But then I looked past the mess to the things I totally *didn't* expect—bills and magazines, a whole bunch of thin circulars boasting pizza prices and going-out-of-business sales.

"What's that?" Macey asked, picking up a flyer about an upcoming local election.

"Mail," Liz said. Bex raised her eyebrows, and Liz lowered her voice. "I got it from the *cabin*," she whispered. "I thought I'd go read it to *him*."

She didn't use Mr. Solomon's name—she didn't dare there, in the middle of the Grand Hall. But we all knew who she meant. When a pair of eighth graders stopped and tried to help us pick everything up, Macey said, "We've got it," in a *There's nothing to see here* tone, and the girls walked on.

"Oh, I'm sure he's very interested in"—Bex reached for a flyer—"the prices of fertilizer at the local feed store."

"It might help." Liz sounded offended, and I couldn't blame her. She had the biggest brain of anyone I knew. She was going to use all of hers to fix Mr. Solomon's. "According to Strouse and Fleinberg, normal interactions, conversations, and activities can stimulate the unconscious mind to . . ."

Liz went on, citing obscure studies and unproven hypotheses, but I'd stopped listening. I was too busy staring down at a padded manila envelope that had fallen to the floor with the rest of the letters. There were Italian stamps and an airmail sticker from France.

"Who's that from?" Bex asked, following my gaze.

My voice was tight and low as I whispered, "Me."

Chapter nineteen

It happened in a flash.

One moment we were staring at an envelope bearing rows of familiar handwriting and a postmark from Rome. The next, Bex was grabbing the package and running between the tables, bolting through the foyer and up the stairs.

She was practically flying. Something was coming over my roommates, pulling them toward my mother's office, and it didn't take a student at spy school to know that that something... was hope.

But Bex hadn't seen the trustees. Macey hadn't heard the deep voices on the phone. Liz didn't know the questions that swirled around me—the ones not even she could answer. They just knew there was a clue, and so they ran faster.

"Bex," I said just as my best friend yelled, "Headmistress," and ran past Gilly's sword in its gleaming case. "Headmistress!" she called again.

"Bex, I think she's—"

My mother's office door flew open.

"Busy," I finished, the word more exhale than whisper.

"What?" Aunt Abby asked, and the look on her face made me skid to a stop, frozen in my tracks. Liz actually ran into me, stumbled, and knocked over a display of hat pins-slash-poisoned daggers that had been used by a Gallagher Girl during the First World War.

Zach reached down and pulled her effortlessly to her feet, but all I could do was stare at Abby, who was coming toward me through the Hall of History. She neither smiled nor joked. "This is not a good time."

"We need to see Headmistress Morgan," Bex said. "We need to talk to both of you."

"Not now." Abby started to turn and go back to my mother's office, but Bex thrust the package toward her.

"This was at the cabin!"

Abby's eyes got wide as she stared down and whispered, "*Rome*."

"Show me," Mom ordered, and Bex laid the package on the coffee table in front of the sofa—the very place where I'd eaten supper almost every Sunday night since I'd started at the Gallagher Academy in the seventh grade. It was a table normally reserved for spaghetti and bad burritos, but that day we all sat staring down at the only real clue we had about my past.

"You found it . . ." Mom started.

"At the cabin," Liz said, answering the unfinished question. "It was with the rest of Mr. Solomon's mail. I guess Cam must have mailed it to him or something."

I felt the couch shift as my aunt sank to take the seat beside me. "That was good, Cam. Smart."

The CoveOps teacher looked proud; the aunt sounded prouder. I know I should have said thank you, but it felt like cheating to accept a compliment I didn't remember earning— like taking credit for somebody else's hard work.

"Cammie," Zach said, "are you *sure* it's your handwriting?"

For a second, the question seemed strange. Zach had been my sorta-boyfriend for a long time, and yet he didn't know what my handwriting looked like. I guess we weren't exactly love-notes-in-the-locker people. We were too busy being terrorists-want-to-kidnap-us people. It's easy to see how one would get in the way of the other.

"Oh," Bex said with a laugh, "it's hers. I'd know that crazy-person scrawl anywhere."

I ran a finger along the words I had absolutely no memory of writing. The postmark was so foreign, so strange. The stamps seemed like works of art.

"It's a package *I* sent from Rome," I said, then laughed softly to myself. "I've always wanted to go to Rome."

How many covert conversations had my roommates and I had in the past three years? How many hours had we spent staring down at some mysterious clue? I couldn't even begin to count. It felt somehow like they'd all been leading up to that moment—that place. We seemed a long, long way from my first boyfriend's garbage.

"I guess we should start by X-raying it," Liz said slowly. "We'll need to scan it for biohazards, of course, and—"

Abby lunged forward, cutting Liz off. She didn't hesitate as she grabbed the package and ripped. Scraps of paper and packing material flew everywhere, but no one said a thing as Abby turned the envelope upside down and dumped the contents onto the table.

"Or we could do that," Liz finished.

I don't know what I'd been expecting, but it seemed a little anticlimactic, to tell you the truth. There were no bombs, no treasure maps where X marked the spot—just a small pile of bracelets, each with thin wires twisted into the words *Bex*, *Liz*, and *Macey*. I reach for each and handed them to my best friends, who gazed down at the delicate wires that spelled their names.

There were two small brown paper packets, the names *Mom* and *Abby* written across them in my familiar scrawl, and I handed them to their new owners, watched them pull out beautiful pendants hung on delicate chains.

The last package was simply labeled *Me*.

I could barely breathe as I tipped the tiny envelope upside down and immediately felt something cool and metal land on my palm. On the end of a very fine chain, I found a small pewter crest almost like the one from the Gallagher Academy, but different. And still it was close enough that I could see why it would catch my eye and make me choose it for myself.

"Well, Cam, I guess you were wrong that day when you came back," Bex said slowly. She held the bracelet up. "You got us something after all."

But I barely heard my best friend's words. I was pushing through the scraps of paper and packing material, searching, but there was nothing else in the pile.

"It's not here," I said.

"What's that, kiddo?" Mom asked me.

"Dad's journal. I hoped maybe I'd sent it back, but it's not here. It's just . . . jewelry," I said. Suddenly, I wanted to hurl the necklace across the room, throw it out the window, do anything but sit there holding proof that I'd been to Rome and had nothing to show for it but some trinkets. For the first time since waking up in Austria, I actually wanted to cry. "It's just stupid souvenirs. It doesn't tell us anything!"

I tried to get up, but Bex was already taking the seat on the arm of the couch beside me, the bracelet around her wrist.

"You didn't just send us souvenirs, Cam," she said, smiling.

"Yeah," Liz agreed. "You sent us souvenirs . . . *from Rome.*"

I think every Gallagher Girl in history has fantasized about the places her job will take her. In my dreams, Bex was beside me, Liz was somewhere running comms. There was usually a prince, a count, and a rogue arms dealer of some sort. And my dream, believe it or not, had always taken place in Rome.

I was in Rome, I had to think. I racked my brain, looking for memories of the Colosseum. I swallowed hard, searching for the taste of truly authentic pizza. It was the kind of thing I shouldn't have been able to forget. The irony was almost too much.

Macey slapped her hands together and turned to my mother. "So when do we leave? I can call Dad's secretary and get a jet here by the end of the day."

I watched Bex and Liz begin to mentally pack and plan as Macey talked about the advantages of private jet travel. Zach and I were the only ones who saw the look that crossed Aunt Abby's face.

I'd only seen that look twice before. Once in my mother's office during Abby's first few days as Macey's guard. Another time on a moving train outside of Philadelphia, barreling through the night. It had been almost a year since I'd seen my aunt wear that expression, and I knew it wasn't anger. There was no rage. It was simply a mixture of guilt and regret so deep that neither word could do it justice.

The only word that came to mind was heartbreak.

"What is it, Abby?" I asked. "What aren't you telling me?"

"Rome . . ." Abby said, just as my mother said, "Abby, no—"

"She has the right to know, Rachel," Abby snapped, but then lowered both her voice and her gaze. "Cam deserves to know that it's all my fault."

"You're wrong," Mom said, but Abby shook her head.

"Am I?"

"What does Rome mean?" Zach asked.

"Someone tell me," I demanded.

"About a month before your father disappeared, he called me," Abby said. "He was excited about something—more excited than I'd heard him in years. He didn't want to tell Joe or even your mother, but he was close to something that could bring the Circle down. Those were his words: 'Bring the Circle down.' And he wanted me to come meet him—to help him. But I was late . . ." She turned to look out the window. "He was calling me from Rome. That's what Rome means."

"Matthew didn't disappear for another four weeks, Abby. My husband *did not* disappear in Rome. It *is not* your fault."

"He wanted me there, Rachel. Whatever it was, he needed me there."

"*So when do we leave?*" Macey said again, fresh emphasis on every word.

"That's the thing, Macey." Zach stood and walked to the bookshelves. "We don't."

Liz looked at him as if he were crazy. "But it's a clue. It's a piece of the puzzle, a—"

"Risk," I finished for her. "It's a big risk." I looked down at the envelope with its frayed edges. "*I'm* a big risk."

"But . . ." Liz sounded utterly confused. "We went to the cabin and we found this. It has to matter. It has to mean something."

"We went to the cabin, and the Circle found *me*." I took a deep breath. "And then I killed someone."

"But . . ." Liz started, and then realized that even she didn't know how that sentence was supposed to end.

"They sent someone to kill her, Liz," Zach said. "And they'll keep sending people until they succeed."

I watched Bex, saw her weighing the risks and rewards in her mind, but my mother was the only one who spoke.

"We're going to have to think about this." She stood, gently cradling in her hands the small packet I'd given her.

"But—" Liz started.

"But they don't need me alive anymore." I started for the door. "Everything is different now that they don't need me alive."

No one told me I was wrong.

"Go to class," Abby said. "We've got a lot to think about."

Chapter Twenty

We left the package in my mother's office, but the memory of it followed us everywhere we went for the rest of the day.

I doodled the postmark all over the back of a pop quiz from Madame Dabney. In Advanced Languages, I kept writing and rewriting the address (but that worked out okay because I was writing it in Swahili).

By the time the day was almost over, there was one thing that I couldn't shake from my mind.

"Who is Zeke Rozell?" I asked, remembering the words on the label.

The classroom was totally empty—just my friends and Zach and me.

"It's one of Joe's aliases," Zach said with a shrug of his shoulders. "Technically, the cabin belongs to Mr. Rozell. He pays taxes and has a valid local driver's license and makes an annual donation to the volunteer fire department, but he works in off-shore drilling, so he doesn't get into town very much."

Bex smiled slowly. "Mr. Solomon is awesome."

"Mr. Solomon is in a coma," I said numbly, sliding into my seat in the almost empty room.

"We know," Macey said, as if the last thing any of us needed was a reminder.

"No. I mean Mr. Solomon is *in a coma*—and I *knew* that. I would have known he wasn't there. Why would I send something to an empty cabin?"

"Because you'd planned on being there to get it." When Bex spoke, it was as though the girl who had shouted at me in the forest was a million miles away, shattered by a sniper's bullet, washed away like the black of my hair down the drain. *"You were coming back,"* she said again, emphasizing every word.

"I was coming back," I repeated as, one by one, the rest of the senior class filtered through the door and took their places all around me.

I barely noticed a thing, though, until I heard Professor Buckingham say, "Good afternoon, ladies. Mr. Goode."

She didn't look like a woman who'd had a clandestine, predawn rendezvous. But then again, I think clandestine rendezvous are probably what Professor Buckingham does best.

"Today our friends at the FBI have asked for a baseline assessment of your proficiency in the following technical maneuvers." She handed a stack of folders to the first girl in every row, and slowly they passed the rest back. "So if you will follow me outside, we will begin . . . Yes, Cameron?" Buckingham said when I raised my hand.

"I don't have one," I said, looking down at the stack in my

hands. Our names were written at the top in bold, black letters, but my name was nowhere to be seen.

"I'm afraid the medical staff has not cleared you for this particular exercise. You will have to sit this one out, dear."

"But I don't want to sit anything out."

"Cameron, I will not be responsible for you re-injuring yourself."

Not twenty-four hours before, I'd been fighting for my life in the woods around Joe Solomon's cabin. No one had cleared me for that, I started to say, but thought better of it at the last minute.

"In the meantime," Professor Buckingham went on, "I believe Dr. Steve has requested a word with you."

My classmates went still, and I felt like the least chameleony girl in the world as I gathered my things and walked outside.

"Oh, Cammie, come in. Come in."

Whatever pain meds Dr. Steve was taking for his shoulder, they must have been the strong ones. I mean the *really* strong ones, because he had gotten two of his shirt buttons in the wrong holes, spilled coffee all over his sling, and he was grinning like he was six years old and someone had just given him a puppy.

"*So* good to see you, Cammie. So *good* to see you," he said over and over, each time emphasizing a different word.

"Uh . . . how are you, Dr. Steve?" I asked.

"Oh, I'm fine, my dear. Perfectly fine. Just a scratch, you know."

I did know, but all I could hear were Zach's words coming back, echoing in my ears: *You could have died. You could have died. You could have—*

"Cammie," Dr. Steve said, jarring me back. "Well, if I didn't know better, I'd say you just took a little trip."

"I'm sorry."

"Don't be. It's perfectly natural for—"

"No, I don't mean sorry for ignoring you. I mean sorry for . . ." I trailed off, but pointed to his sling. "I'm sorry."

"You shouldn't be sorry, Cammie," Dr. Steve said. "I don't know what I would have done if you'd been hurt." A darkness covered his face. He shivered as if the thought were simply too much, and then he forced himself to smile. "Now, tell me, how do you feel?"

"I'm fine."

"No, Cammie"—he shook his head slowly—"how do you *feel?*" And then I knew he wasn't talking about my bruises or my scars or even the knot that was growing steadily smaller on my head. He was the one who'd been shot, but Dr. Steve knew that I might have been the one seriously wounded on that hillside.

"I killed a man," I said.

"Yes, you did."

"He was going to stab Bex, so . . . I killed him."

"And how does that make you feel?"

It was an excellent question—one the Gallagher Academy had never really taught me how to answer. I was tired and confused, guilty and relieved. But most of all, I felt nothing. And nothing, as it turns out, is one of the scariest feelings of all.

When I finally got back to the suite that night, I was greeted by a single sentence and three scorching looks.

"Where were you?"

"Why?" I asked, closing the door and dropping my books on the bed. I sat down and tried to pull off my shoes, but Macey was looming over me.

"It's almost ten," she explained.

"Wow. I guess I lost track of time. I was in the library."

Bex looked at Liz. "I thought you looked in the library."

Liz's eyes were wide. "I did."

The three of them turned as if they'd just caught me in an elaborate lie—like I'd run away again that afternoon but hadn't bothered to tell them.

"I was in the stacks doing that makeup exam for Mr. Mosckowitz," I said, but they were still staring at me. "I swear."

I held up a hand, Scout's-honor style, and Bex eased forward, slowly shaking her head. "Now's not the time for disappearing acts, okay?"

"Okay," I said, meaning it. All over the floor there were papers and charts and note cards. It was exactly what I'd always imagined the inside of Liz's head to look like. "What's all this?"

"Rome," Liz said, as if that single word were an all-encompassing answer to my question.

I pointed to the line on a flip chart that just read MACEY in capital letters.

Macey shrugged. "I have a jet," she said, because, I guess, "free jet" is an asset that should never be undervalued.

"Guys, that's awesome, but I can't go to Rome. You know that, right?"

"But . . ." Macey started, then trailed off, pointed at her name. "*Jet.*"

I wanted to tell them that no number of flash cards could change the fact that the Gallagher Academy was the one place where I was safe. I didn't dare say that I was terrified that if I left our walls, the trustees might never agree to let me back in. Even then, in the quiet stillness of our room, I couldn't bring myself to relive the words I'd heard the trustees utter, so I just shook my head.

"I'm never leaving again."

"Fine. So you can't go. But *we* can." Bex pointed from herself to Liz and Macey.

"What exactly are you guys going to do? Wander around the streets of Rome with my picture, asking if anybody saw me bump my head?"

"We have a lead, Cam," Liz said. "This is a good thing." She picked up the bracelet that spelled out her name. "This is—"

"A trinket. A souvenir. It's *nothing.*"

"Oh, not nothing," Macey said. She held her thin wrist out

so that her bracelet caught the light. "I saw something just like it in the September *Vogue*."

Amazingly, that made me feel better. "Well, at least I'm a crazy person with good taste."

"We'll figure it out, Cam," Liz said, hugging me, then climbing into her bed. "I hacked into the security feeds of all the airports and train stations in southern Italy. And I've got a worm working its way through the customs office database, running facial recognition software and . . . I promise we'll figure it out."

Even in the twin-size bed, Liz looked tiny, lying there with her covers pulled up to her chin. I wanted to keep her safe, protect them all. And for the first time since I got back, I wondered if they would have been better off if I had just kept running.

"Cam . . ." Macey's voice brought me back. "You're doing it again."

"Doing what?"

"Singing that song."

"I'm sorry," I said with a shake of my head. Liz's eyes were closed, and Bex was in the bathroom. Macey and I were utterly alone when she looked at me.

"Where did you go?"

"That's a good question," I told her, and then I tried to go to sleep.

That night, when my dreams came, they came in Italian. There were dark alleys and faceless people lurking in the shadows of my mind. I grabbed for the bracelets, but my wrists were bare.

The necklace around my neck seemed to burn. And when I jolted awake, my hand grappled with it, half expecting to feel a scar.

My first thought was: *Where am I?*, but the soft sheets were familiar beneath my hands. My legs were tangled in the covers, keeping me there even as my mind ran down cobblestone streets. I lay back down on the bed and forced myself to breathe. To think. It was just a dream. It was only a . . .

There was a sound then, soft and light, and I spun to see a figure searching my closet in the dark. Not any of my roommates. Not Zach.

Abby.

I blinked twice just to make sure my messed-up mind wasn't seeing things, but there was no mistaking the woman who turned to me, an empty duffel bag in her hands. "Get packed," she whispered, and tossed the bag onto my bed. "Get dressed." She started for the door. "We leave in twenty minutes."

Okay, I know I was half asleep and brain damaged and all, but that seriously didn't sound like the suggestion of someone who was convinced that I would never be allowed to leave my school again.

I threw off the covers and followed her into the hall.

"Abby—" I started.

"Come on, Squirt. Clock's ticking. Spies are fast packers. Consider it your CoveOps lesson for the day." She gestured to the door. "Now, go. And be quiet. We don't want to wake—"

"Us?" Bex's voice sounded even more mischievous than

usual when she appeared in the doorway and crossed her arms, then turned to the girl behind her. "What do you think, Macey? I think she's talking about us."

But Abby didn't answer. She just glared at me. "I said pack and dress *quietly*."

"It's not Cam's fault," Bex told her. "We rigged her bed so that if she gets up, I get an electric shock."

"Liz designed it," Macey said, and Bex shrugged.

"We told you we were taking precautions."

Of course. Because at the Gallagher Academy, "precautions" usually equals "voluntary shock therapy."

"So we're leaving?" Macey asked, following Bex into the hallway. Despite the hour, there was a brightness in her blue eyes.

"*We're* not going anywhere," Abby snapped. "Cam, you now have ten minutes to get ready. Bex, you and Macey have ten seconds to go back to bed."

"No," Macey said, almost whining. For the first time in years, she actually sounded like the bored, spoiled heiress she was when she'd come to us.

"Yes," Abby countered in an identical tone. Watching the two of them square off gave me an acute case of déjà vu, remembering when Abby had been Macey's Secret Service agent—when Abby had taken a bullet meant for Macey.

Abby had taken a bullet . . .

"Go to bed, guys." My voice was flat and even.

"But—"

"But no one else is getting hurt," I said, cutting Bex off.

"Abby?" Mom appeared at the end of the hallway. She didn't seem at all surprised to see us up. And arguing.

"They hot-wired Cam's bed," Abby said with a shrug.

"Of course they did," my mother said.

"You've got to take us with you," Macey said, but it wasn't a plea. It was more a statement of fact.

"And why is that?" Mom asked.

"We know Cammie," Macey said. "You need us to help you figure out where she went and what she did."

"Yeah," Bex agreed. "And you're not going through official channels on this, are you?"

Mom and Abby shared a glance, which was answer enough for Bex.

"Of course you aren't. You can't risk telling Langley. The Circle has way too many moles at the CIA. And the more people who know, the more likely you are to have a repeat of what happened at the cabin, so you aren't telling anyone, and you aren't taking any backup. We're alone now. We are all alone."

"I wouldn't say that, girls," Abby said. "I'll have some backup."

"You're not taking enough," Bex countered. She sounded very much like Abby's equal. "If we were underclassmen, sure. Maybe. We would have argued, but we would have been wrong. But now we're a semester and a half away from being field-qualified, and we've already seen more real-world ops than most new graduates see in five years."

"You *need* backup," Macey said, stepping forward. "We can *be* backup. Don't make us stay here like we're . . . helpless." Her voice cracked, and right then I knew that I might have been the one who'd gotten a concussion last summer, but I wasn't the only one who'd gotten hurt.

"Girls." Mom shook her head. "What about Liz?"

"I'll stay." Liz was standing in the doorway in her frilliest, pinkest nightgown, looking exactly like Doris Day in a very old movie. "Bex and Macey should go, but I can stay and help with ground support and research and . . . Bex and Macey *should* go." She took a deep breath, and then Elizabeth Sutton, the smartest girl at the Gallagher Academy for Exceptional Young Women, looked at our headmistress and said, "The odds of bringing her back alive increase by twenty-seven percent if Bex and Macey go."

I don't know if it's a spy thing or a sister thing, but sometimes my mom and Aunt Abby can have whole conversations without saying a single word. Looks pass between them, thoughts move through the air like some kind of encrypted transmission. I watched them having one of those talks then. And still I had no idea what the verdict would be until Abby wheeled on Bex and Macey.

"Fine," she said. "You two can come."

"Awesome," Bex said. She turned and started to run down the hall. "I'll get Zach and—"

"Not Zach."

Bex stopped and spun at the sound of my mother's voice. Mom looked at Abby, then added, "Cammie isn't the only person the Circle would like back. Zach stays here."

"Don't worry, Squirt," Aunt Abby said. "We have you covered."

I looked at Bex and Macey and then back to my aunt Abby, unable to hide the skepticism in my voice. "Who exactly is *we*?"

"That would be me, young lady."

A tall, broad figure appeared in the shadows of the hall behind Aunt Abby, and I knew the British accent and mildly condescending tone as soon as I heard them. Agent Townsend smiled and picked up the heavy bag that sat at my aunt's feet, then threw it over his shoulder as if it weighed nothing at all.

"Let's go."

Chapter twenty-one

PROS AND CONS OF INTERNATIONAL
TRAVEL AS A SEMI-FUGITIVE:
(A list by Cameron Morgan with help from
Rebecca Baxter and Macey McHenry)

PRO: Macey McHenry was right—private jets are awesome.

CON: Leaving in the middle of the night to make sure no one sees you can seriously disrupt a girl's sleep cycles.

PRO: Two words: no customs.

CON: Madame Dabney had promised to begin Wednesday's lecture with the story of how she once infiltrated an Irish Republican Army stronghold using nothing but dental floss and a batch of homemade scones.

CON: Packing at one a.m. pretty much guarantees a person will end up with socks that don't match, a pair of jeans that don't fit, and the sweatshirt with the big bleach stain on the elbow.

CON: Watching the stone walls of your school fade into the distance, your mother behind them.

PRO: Hoping that answers might lie beyond.

CON: Being a semi-fugitive means guards. And sometimes the guards include Agent Townsend.

PRO: Realizing that Agent Townsend is seriously not a match for Abigail Cameron.

————

"Cam, don't sit there," my aunt told me an hour later, pointing at the window seat I was already halfway into.

"Stay where you are, Ms. Morgan," Agent Townsend ordered. "I don't think there are a lot of snipers at thirty thousand feet over the Atlantic."

"Yes," Abby countered, "because obviously a plane is never on the ground, like it is . . . say . . . *now*."

"Oh, please." Townsend shrugged off her worries. "If they know she's on this plane, they'll simply shoot the whole thing down."

"Oh," Bex and I said at the same time.

Not. A. Comforting. Thought.

Maybe that was where the feeling in my gut was coming from. Knowing the Circle wanted me alive had been terrifying. Knowing the Circle wanted me dead and didn't care who died with me was a whole new level of fear.

"You get some sleep, Abigail," Townsend told her. "I'll keep watch."

"That's very gracious of you, but being that we're *on an airplane...*"

Even after the plane took off, they kept debating security perimeters and protocols. I'm pretty sure they argued for forty-five minutes about where the best place for cappuccino was near the Colosseum.

Finally Townsend said, "Always a loose cannon, aren't you, Abigail? Taking chances."

"I seem to remember one of those chances saving your hide in Buenos Aires three years ago."

"Oh, Abigail... still bringing up Buenos Aires?"

"Well, you're still alive because of it."

It should have been easy to curl up in the plush leather seat and rest. (Grandma Morgan has always claimed that I am a world-class sleeper.) But every time I closed my eyes, I heard the music floating through my mind, the new soundtrack to my life. I turned my head to the window, but all I saw was the image of the sniper's knife reflected in the darkened glass.

Finally, I tried to feign sleep. I would have sworn it didn't work, but five minutes later, someone shook my shoulder.

I bolted upright and grabbed the hand that held me, twisted the wrist backward at an impossible angle. It was a second too late before I realized the hand was semi-friendly.

"Not bad, Ms. Morgan," Townsend said, unfazed. He didn't seem to be in even a little pain as he freed himself and told me, "Get your shoes on. We're here."

* * *

Somewhere over the Atlantic, Abby and Townsend must have called a truce. Or arm wrestled. Or compromised, because it was impossible to tell who'd won. They both seemed equally unhappy with our arrangement as I climbed down the stairs of the plane and onto the sunny tarmac below.

"You're with me, Cammie." Aunt Abby looped her arm through mine in a gesture that had nothing to do with girlie bonding. It was more like, *They'll have to go through me to get to you.*

Townsend had arranged for a van, and the five of us crawled inside like a totally dysfunctional family. Townsend drove.

"Via del Corso is faster," Abby said in a singsong voice. Townsend ignored her.

I sat in the back, wedged between Bex and Macey, staring at cobblestone streets lined with ancient buildings. There were bicycles and old women selling flowers, scooters and police cars that drove through the city with haunting, piercing sirens that caused the hair on my arms to stand on end. But nothing felt familiar.

"Anything, Cam?" Macey asked, turning to me.

I shook my head. "I think I need to walk."

"Not here," Abby and Townsend said at the same time. There was something especially terrifying about hearing them agree.

"But Dr. Steve says that music and sensory stimuli are essential in memory recall."

"I've never heard him say that," Bex said.

"Well . . . he told me," I said.

Townsend shrugged. "With all due respect to the good doctor, I highly suspect that he's a moron."

That didn't sound very respectful, but it hardly seemed like the moment to say so. And besides, there wasn't time, because Agent Townsend was parking the van and announcing, "We're here."

It was a street just like a dozen others we'd seen since reaching the city center. Laundry lines ran between windows, a floating cloud of shirts and sheets.

"We're *where?*" Bex asked, but then Townsend turned and pointed at the place where dozens of tourists were bleeding onto one street from another.

"There," he said, just as Abby opened her door and laughing and talking filled the air. A large truck pulled away from the curb, and I caught a glimpse of brightly colored fabrics waving in the wind. There were stacks upon stacks of pashminas, rows of belts and piles of purses so high that I could smell the scent of leather in the air. People haggled over jewelry and imitation Michelangelos, and through it all, I kept thinking, *I came here?*

"Not so fast," Townsend told me when I reached for the door. He pulled a bulletproof vest from the back of the van. "You're a little underdressed."

My aunt must have felt my hesitation, because she turned to take my hand. "Your mom and Liz and the five of us are the only ones who know you're here. We're the only ones who know about the package and the jewelry, so it's highly unlikely that the Circle has staked out this place like they did the cabin." She squeezed my hand. Townsend might have rolled his eyes.

"You're here so we can get the Circle, Ms. Morgan. If you want to do something that has absolutely no risk, then you should have stayed at your little school and saved us all a lot of trouble."

He was right, of course. The only way to be safe was for all of this to be over. The only way for it to be over was to put the vest on and climb out of the van.

Chapter Twenty-two

Covert Operations Report

On the eleventh of October, Operatives Morgan, Baxter, and McHenry engaged in a highly classified reconnaissance operation on the streets of Rome, Italy.

Agents Townsend and Cameron showed The Operatives how to form a close-range perimeter around Operative Morgan.

The Operatives also got to eat really awesome gelato for breakfast.

By the time we made it halfway through the market, I was starting to regret quoting Dr. Steve. Seriously. At that point I didn't want any more sensory stimuli. What I wanted was for someone to turn the color and smells and volume down.

Cobblestones were beneath my feet. I ran my fingers against the rough stucco of the buildings' walls, but nothing felt familiar. Even my own shadow was unrecognizable, with my shorter hair and bulletproof-vested physique.

Bex gave me a wink, and for a second I thought about Zach. I know this probably makes me the worst unofficial girlfriend ever, but it was kind of nice not having him there. It felt good to be just us girls again. It was nice to have the chance to miss him.

Townsend slipped his arm around my shoulders. Made by anyone else, it would have been a fatherly motion, a kind gesture. But I knew there was nothing sweet about it. It was just a really hard position to attack.

"Crowds are difficult," I told him.

He nodded. "They are."

"The number of potential threats, coupled with the decreased line of sight . . ." I went on, thinking about the cabin and the shooter and how close I'd come to dying on that hillside.

"It's different from an attack in a secluded area," Townsend said, as if he'd read my mind. "But not necessarily harder."

Abby was two feet in front of us, clearing the way through the crowd, but somehow I knew I wasn't in Rome with the best possible people—not with Mr. Solomon lying in a bed in the Gallagher Academy. The best possible person might never stand or speak or challenge me again.

"Ask me what I see," I heard myself blurting.

"Excuse me?" Townsend asked, taken aback.

"It's a test," I told him, the words coming fast. "It should be a test. I've been trained for this. I know . . . Ask me what I see!"

"Very well, Ms. Morgan." We'd reached a place in the

market where the streets branched and the crowds were thinner. He released my shoulders and stepped slightly away. "What do you see?"

I took a deep breath and told myself that it was just another school assignment. There was no difference between that busy foreign street and the Roseville town square. It was just another Wednesday.

I turned and looked, saw a vendor selling cashmere gloves and heavy coats. I smelled freshly roasted nuts, and in the distance, someone was playing a guitar, picking out a song with words I didn't know. It was the kind of place a person might go to fall in love; but Zach was on another continent, and my mind was totally supposed to be on other things.

I closed my eyes and tried to imagine the hot sun on my skin. I mentally changed the bulletproof vest for a tank top, my sneakers for sandals. A sweet taste lingered on my tongue, and part of me knew that I'd tasted the gelato before—that I'd sworn to come back and try that place again.

"Take your time, Cam," Bex said, and I opened my eyes just as the crowd parted, and I found myself staring at an old woman in a stall twenty feet away.

"Ah, *signorina*," the old woman said to Macey, reaching for her arm. Abby moved to block her way, but then the old woman saw me. She stopped and stared and said, "So you did come back."

It took me a moment to register that she was speaking in Italian.

And she was speaking to me.

"Your friends"—she gestured to Bex and Macey—"they like very much?"

"What are you talking about?" I moved toward her too quickly. I could tell she was afraid, but I couldn't slow down as I blurted, "How do you know me? What—"

"Cam." Bex's voice cut me off. "Look," she said, pointing to the jewelry that filled the woman's booth. Necklaces and earrings and bracelets—hundreds of bracelets exactly like the ones my best friends wore.

"I make myself," the old woman said. Her English was broken and heavily accented. "You look so lovely, *signorina*." She patted her hair as if to say that something was different. "I like. Shows your pretty face."

I had been there. I'd had long hair, and I had been there.

"When?" Macey pushed me aside to ask the question. "When was she here?" she said again, this time in Italian.

The old woman looked at her as if she were crazy not to just ask me, but then she shrugged and answered. "It was July, I think. Very hot." She fanned herself and turned to me. "Very busy day, but you waited. You and your young man."

For a moment I was sure I must have been hearing things. The crowded streets were too loud, my head too broken. But the words were still there, echoing down the cobblestones.

Me and my young man.

"What . . . what does it mean?" Macey asked.

"It means Cammie was here," Townsend said simply.

"And I wasn't alone."

Chapter twenty-three

Abby must have been the one who found the safe house, because Townsend didn't like it.

"The building across the street is under construction," he snarled as soon as we'd carried our bags inside.

"The elevator has key card access, and I've hacked into the surveillance cameras from every system on the block," Abby argued. "We have a three-hundred-sixty-degree visual."

"Excellent." Townsend dropped his bag. "Now the Circle can see us from every angle."

"Don't mind Agent Townsend, girls," Abby told us. "He's a glass-half-empty kind of spy."

"Also known as the good kind," he countered. Abby huffed.

"That's a matter of opinion," she said, but Townsend either didn't hear or didn't care. He just went to check the windows of the small apartment, mumbling about inferior locks and closed-circuit TVs as he went.

There were only four rooms in the flat, a living room with galley kitchen, two bedrooms, and one bath. Abby pointed to the door that led to the largest bedroom in the back. "You're in there. It's time for you three to get some sleep."

"But I'm not sleepy," Bex said.

"Doesn't matter. We lost six hours in flight, and now it's bedtime." Abby cocked a hip. "Jet lag—it's killed more spies than anthrax. Now, go. Townsend and I will take shifts. We need the three of you rested." Abby grabbed a duffel and headed down the narrow hall. "Meanwhile, I'm going to call in."

I didn't follow. I just stayed in the dim living room, listening to my aunt's voice, soft and low, coming from the other room. Somewhere in the apartment, water was running. I could imagine Macey washing her face, Bex brushing her teeth. The smart thing would have been to do exactly as my aunt had told me and at least try to rest, but I was both too wired and too exhausted to sleep. Rome was right outside our window, and through the glass, the city called to me. It felt like we were playing a very strange, very high-stakes game of hide-and-seek, and I didn't have a clue where Summer Me might have been hiding.

"It's probably best not to stand next to the window, Ms. Morgan."

"I know," I said, the words coming out harder than I'd intended. "I'm sorry. I didn't mean to snap. I guess—"

"It's okay, Cammie. I know that you know. Your aunt hasn't ruined you entirely. Yet."

And then, in the reflection in the glass, I could have sworn I saw Agent Townsend smile. It was the closest thing to a compliment I'd ever heard him give. And even though it wasn't much of one, I was willing to take it.

"Why are you doing this?" I asked, the question taking me by surprise. "Why are you . . . helping me?"

"You assume that helping you is why I'm here." The man leaned against the wall and crossed his arms. "Perhaps I have ulterior motives."

"Oh," I said, and then I couldn't help it: the words of MI6 and the CIA, the trustees, and even my own mother were coming back to me in a flood. "Is it because I'm dangerous?"

"It is." He didn't try to soften the words, cushion the blow. He just pushed away from the wall and added, "But not in the way you think you are."

When Townsend pulled aside the heavy curtain, the glow of the streetlights sliced across his face, highlighting dark stubble and striking blue eyes.

"Whatever is in your mind, Ms. Morgan, the Circle has devoted a great many resources to getting it—and now to making sure no one else can have it. That makes it something I would very much like to have. And that makes *you* someone I would very much like to protect."

He had the quiet, confident gaze of a truly great operative, and it felt a little like I was looking at Zach . . . in the future. I remembered why, once upon a time, for about a second and a half, I'd thought Agent Townsend was dreamy.

"You can have it." I couldn't help myself; I smiled. "If we figure out what it is, I'll totally give it to you."

He smiled back. "Deal."

I could hear Abby on the phone, her voice floating toward us from the other room.

"Now go to sleep, Ms. Morgan. That aunt of yours is difficult enough when things go according to plan."

Someone had boarded up the windows of the bedroom and brought in three small mattresses. Macey and Bex were each sitting on one, and Abby paced between them, a satellite phone to her ear.

"She's right here, Rachel," Abby said. She rolled her eyes, then nodded. "Yes, I'm looking at her. Ha-ha."

She sounded like a kid sister, and for about the zillionth time in my life, I regretted being an only child. But then Macey threw a pillow at Bex, and I realized that maybe "only child" was just a technicality.

"You want to talk to her?" Abby asked me, but of all the things I wanted to say to my mother, none of them would help, so I shook my head and sank onto an empty mattress.

"She's in bed," Abby told her sister. "Yeah," she said, nodding. "Uh-huh. Of course. Yeah, well you can tell Townsend—Why is everyone forgetting about Buenos Aires?!" She threw her hand in the air, and my friends and I had to bite back a laugh. "Yeah," Abby said, after a long time. "Don't worry. She isn't leaving our sight."

Finally, Abby hung up the phone. Only then did I notice the way that Bex and Macey were sitting, straight up on their beds. Waiting, listening.

"What's going on?" I asked, searching their eyes for some kind of clue.

"Just checking in with your mom, Squirt." There was no worry in Abby's voice. No fear. It was exactly how she was supposed to sound. She gave me a quick wink and closed the door, and my only thought was *Aunt Abby is the Best Liar Ever.*

"Tell me," I said, turning to Bex.

"Don't be silly, Cam. For a totally unofficial mission, this thing is going way better than—"

I turned and set my sights on Macey. "What is it?"

"It's nothing," she said.

"So there *is* an 'it'?" I asked.

Macey looked like I'd just kicked her in the stomach. I turned back to Bex, who shrugged and said, "It's *probably* nothing."

"You know who I was with, don't you?" I asked, standing and moving toward her, but she was already up and meeting me halfway. "You know!"

"Shh. Do you want Townsend busting in here?" she asked, but I talked on.

"I've told you everything I know, and now the two of you are holding out on me?"

Interrogation tactics, I learned from Mr. Solomon. Guilt, I got from Grandma Morgan. It must have worked, too, because in the next moment, Macey was saying, "I trust Zach, Cam. I know his mom is evil and all, but I know evil parents. And I know you don't have to end up like them, so I trust Zach."

I stood there listening to the words, but they didn't quite make sense.

"Uh . . . okay," I told her. "But Zach was with Bex last summer."

"Not *with me* with me," Bex clarified.

"Yeah," I said, almost ashamed of where I'd allowed my mind to go just days before. "Of course. He was with your—"

"And not all summer," Bex said, staring down at her hands.

"Bex," I spoke slowly, surely, "tell me everything you know."

In the living room, Townsend and Abby were arguing again, their voices floating through the wall; but the only words that mattered were Bex's.

"After you left and school was out, your mom was going crazy, and Mr. Solomon was . . . sick. So my mom said Zach should come to London—that'd he'd be safe with us." Bex shook her head slowly. "Everything was crazy. *Everyone* was crazy."

"Bex, I know."

"No," Macey snapped. "You don't. Remember when *I* ran away? Well, multiply that by about a thousand and then *maybe* you'll start to understand."

She was right, but that didn't mean I had to say so.

"What does this have to do with Zach?"

"People go crazy in different ways," Bex said with a shrug. "Liz took up baking—almost burned her parents' house to the ground. But Zach . . . well, the two of you really are a lot alike, because Zach . . . ran away."

"So . . ." I thought about the look in the old woman's eyes, the words echoing in my mind: *your young man*. "So he might have found me."

I know it sounds weak and all, but the truth is, I had to lie down. Maybe it was the lingering effects of being too thin and too banged up for my own good, but it was more like the words were too heavy for me.

"What does that mean?" I stared up at Bex. "What does it mean—that he found me and then . . . left me? Or I left him . . . Or—"

"He was only gone two weeks and then he *came back*," Bex said, almost pleading with me not to jump to terrible conclusions.

"But maybe, in the meantime, he'd found me," I said.

"No," Macey said. "He didn't."

"You don't know that," I told her.

"No, but I know boys." She exhaled a half-laugh. "And I know liars. And when school started, Zach was as in the dark about where you were and where you'd been as anyone."

"We've got to call Mom," I said. "We've got to call her and have her *ask him* where he went."

"We did," Bex said. There was a strange light in her eyes when she said, "He told us he went looking for you."

"What aren't you telling me?" I asked, far too tired of secrets.

"Nothing," Macey said, easing onto the mattress beside me. "There is absolutely nothing else you need to know."

She looked totally convincing—sounded totally convincing. But I wasn't convinced. Maybe it was the spy in me. Or maybe I just didn't believe anything anymore.

Chapter twenty-four

That night, even as I slept, I saw the city streets. They were emptier than I remembered, though. Too dark. Too cold. Something pulled me forward, down a path I didn't know. And beneath it all, there was a word that kept washing over me, breaking against me like a wave.

Cammie.

Cammie.

Cammie.

It was Zach's voice calling to me through the haze.

Cammie.

I heard it drawing closer, and so I fled, past closed doors and heavy gates. The fog grew thicker, and I ran.

"Cammie, wait!" Zach yelled, but I couldn't trust the words. Didn't trust my own mind. There were sirens and horns and the feel of the wind.

"Cammie, stop!" he yelled.

Another horn. The rush of air.

"Cammie!"

And then arms grabbed me, pulled me from my feet. I wanted to hit and claw and keep running, but my feet no longer struck the pavement. I tried to toss and turn—to break free— but the covers must have been tangled around me. There was no escape.

"No," I said to myself, panting. "No. No. No."

"Cammie!" Zach's voice was stronger. I began to shake. "Gallagher Girl, wake up!"

"No, no," I said, certain I could stop the dream. Change it. I was so sure there were answers at the end of that dark walk, and I had to stay there—stay sleeping to find them.

"Cammie!"

My back slammed into a wall, and only then did I bolt awake.

A car horn screamed out. The wind I felt was the rushing air of the passing traffic as Zach held me on a narrow sidewalk.

"Cammie, are you okay?" he asked, searching my eyes. "Cammie, wake up," he shouted, shaking me again. "Tell me you're okay. Tell me—"

"Where am I?" I asked, but then the last day came rushing back to me. I knew where I was, and most of all, who I was supposed to be with. "Zach?"

"Cammie, are you hurt?"

"Why are *you* here, Zach? Why aren't you at school? Why are you . . ." I remembered Abby's hushed conversation behind closed doors, the look that had passed between Macey and Bex when I'd asked why my mom couldn't just *ask* Zach where he'd gone last summer.

"You ran away." I wasn't sure if I was talking about now or about last summer. It didn't really matter.

"I was worried about you." He glanced up and down at the dark street. "Looks like I was right to."

"So you just . . . left?"

Zach huffed. "All the cool kids are doing it."

When he reached for me, I pulled away, started to go back the way I'd come. Then I realized I had no idea which way that was. I was wearing Macey's shoes and Bex's jeans and a T-shirt with a tear on the sleeve. My hair was blowing all around my face. Sleep clung to the corners of my eyes, and I had no idea how far I'd wandered through the night.

"Cammie, what are you doing—"

"I don't know, okay?" My voice echoed down the street, and I hated those words almost as much as I hated the Circle.

"Come on." Zach gripped my hand. "We've got to get you back to Abby before she—"

"Were you here with me, Zach?" I couldn't look at him when I said it. "Last summer . . ."

"What are you talking about, Gallagher Girl?"

"I know you left the Baxters'. I know you ran away. And . . . I know I was in Rome. And I wasn't alone."

"Someone else was with you?" The first look that filled his face was shock, as if he'd heard me wrong. And then the expression shifted into a simmering rage. "Someone was *with you*?"

"Tell me, Zach." I don't know if it was the wind or the adrenaline, but I shivered. "And don't lie to me."

"I'm not lying!" he snapped, then took a deep breath. "Last summer, I *did* go looking for you. And when I couldn't find you, I went looking for *my mom*. And that's not exactly something I'm proud of."

When I shivered again, Zach took off his coat and tried to slip it around my shoulders, but I pushed his arm away.

"Don't," I said.

"Listen to me." He grabbed my arms, holding me there. "I couldn't find you. And I will never forgive myself for that. Ever."

Another car passed, and a new fear filled Zach's eyes. The sun was coming up. Light crept over the horizon, and I didn't want to think about the people who might be trying to find me—both the good guys and the bad. Zach must have thought it too, because he grabbed my hand.

"We're getting you out of here." He started to pull, but when we passed the opening of a narrow alley, I had to stop.

"This way," I said, pointing down the dark path.

"No, Cam, you're turned around. I followed you for six blocks, and I was the one who was conscious. Trust me, the safe house is—"

"I have to go this way," I said and pulled harder, breaking free.

I don't know how to describe it. I wasn't in a trance, and I wasn't afraid, but my feet were finding their own path as if pulled by some invisible string.

"Two. One. Nine," I said, the words drifting through my mind.

"I don't like this position, Gallagher Girl," Zach said with a glance around the narrow space.

"Four. Seven. Six," I went on.

"Come on. We've got to get you back to the safe house."

"*Two.*" The word was barely more than a breath.

Zach reached for me, but my hand was already moving, reaching out for the wall on my left, fingers grazing over the mortar until I found a small steel door painted the same color as the stone. I pressed, and the tiny door popped open, revealing a key pad that was hidden inside.

I eased forward, needing to touch the pad, tap out a code I hadn't realized I knew.

"Two-one-nine-four-seven-six-two," I said again, and two feet away, a solid metal door opened like an entrance into another world.

I had to go inside. The door was like a magnet, pulling me close. But before I could cross the threshold, the whole world went upside down. Literally.

I was dangling over Zach's shoulder, and he was bolting down the alley, cursing under his breath and warning me he wasn't in the mood to fight.

"But Zach, I—"

"I don't care," he snapped.

He didn't slow down when I yelled, "Zach, let me go!"

In fact, he didn't stop at all until a tall figure appeared in the alley in front of us, and a voice said, "Cammie? Is that you?"

Chapter twenty-five

The last time I'd seen Preston Winters had been the night his father lost the race for president—the night the Circle had come for me the second time. Or so I thought. As I slid from Zach's shoulder and found my footing, something told me I might have been wrong about that.

When Preston sighed and said, "I guess you did come back," I was certain.

Standing there in jogging pants and a T-shirt, with earbuds dangling around his neck, Preston looked taller and . . . well . . . hotter than I remembered. Despite the chilly air, sweat beaded on his neck. There was a subtle confidence about him, and something in the way he looked at me was enough to tell me that I was finally face-to-face with the boy who'd been by my side last summer.

"Thank goodness you're okay." Preston opened his arms and stepped toward me, but Zach lunged between us.

"That's close enough," he said, and Preston laughed.

Yes, actual *laughage*.

Zach, however, didn't seem to think any of it was funny.

"Sorry," Preston said after a moment. "*You* must be Zach." He held out his hand. "I keep forgetting we haven't been formally introduced. I'm Preston."

But Zach just looked at the hand as if he couldn't decide whether to shake it or break it, so Preston pulled it slowly back to his side.

"Cam told me all about you. But it looks like she hasn't told you about me." Preston gave an exaggerated sigh. "I guess the summer didn't mean anything to you, Cammie. And here I thought I'd made an impression."

There's something about Preston Winters. He has a sort of self-deprecating manner that all really hot nerds are either born with or acquire over time. He laughed, and I waited for it to trigger some feeling inside of me; but the only memory that came had red-white-and-blue bunting and took place totally within the USA.

"So"—he reached for the door I'd just opened and started to walk inside—"I guess you remembered the code?"

I wanted to say something, to beg and plead for answers, but all I managed to do was shake my head and admit, "No. I really didn't."

He turned slowly toward me. Confusion filled his eyes. He didn't look at me like I was crazy. He looked like he was scared.

Of course, it also could have had something to do with

the armed man who was barreling down the alley, screaming, "Freeze!"

Zach was the first to react. In a flash, he was turning to me, yelling, "Run!"

He didn't know that the man in the alley was Agent Townsend. He didn't care that Agent Townsend was heading straight for him.

"Zach, no!" I yelled, then jumped in between the two of them. "Stop!" I cried, but Zach was already grabbing me around the waist and setting me in what he thought was a safer position.

"Ms. Morgan," Townsend snapped. "Go!"

"You're *both* telling me to run!" I screamed while Preston peeked out from behind the door to watch two highly trained fighters in their prime behave like a couple of idiots.

I don't want to think about how long it might have lasted if it hadn't been for the whistle. High and loud, it pierced the air and reverberated in the narrow space for what felt like forever.

Everyone turned and looked through the early morning haze at Bex, who said, "If you boys want to beat each other's guts out, I'm willing to let you, but I'd rather get Cam someplace safe and find out what she's doing walking the streets at five in the bloody morning." She started back down the alley, then stopped and added, "Oh, and Zach, if you're going to run away from school, leave a note. Even Cam did that."

Abby was there, too, Macey by her side. I felt Townsend's

hand on my waist, pushing me down the alley and back to the safe house. Nobody seemed to notice or care about the other boy—the one in the corner, away from the chaos, until Macey stopped.

She didn't sound like herself when she said, "Preston?"

I don't know if it was because she was seeing him, or seeing him hot and sweaty (both in the literal and figurative senses), but I could tell she was thrown in a way no Gallagher Girl is ever supposed to be. "Preston, is that you?"

Then Abby was beside me. She looked from Preston to the buildings that surrounded us, as if trying to place something in her mental map.

"Is this..." she started, looking at the boy, who nodded slowly.

Somehow, Preston didn't seem nearly as freaked out as he should have been when he told us, "I think we need to go inside."

He didn't ask for introductions. No one had to present clearance levels or ID. It was as if Preston knew that being in that alley at that moment meant that you were okay to invite home. Even when home was technically the United States embassy for the ambassador stationed in Rome.

So Preston didn't hesitate. He just led our crazy band through the secret door, and then to another that cordoned off the hallway inside. He stopped to punch out the code my subconscious had remembered.

"You really ought to change that more often," I said as the door popped open.

He smiled. "Will do."

When we reached another door, Preston looked up at a surveillance camera that hung overhead. He gave his loopy grin and a small wave, and a second later, the door buzzed and a uniformed marine pushed it open.

"Welcome back, sir," the marine said. If he was surprised to see Preston appear with three girls, a boy, and two grown-ups, he didn't show it.

Preston pointed to the elevator. "Clear us through to the residence, okay?"

"Yes, sir," the guard said, and a moment later we were all inside an elevator with a marble floor and mirrored walls. A chandelier of Murano glass hung overhead.

"Cool place," Bex told Preston under her breath.

"That's the thing about having a dad who runs for president." Preston gave an awkward smile. "Even losing has its privileges." He took us all in, but really, he had eyes only for Macey. "It's good to see you, Mace."

Bex and I looked at each other. *He calls her Mace?*

"Hi," Macey said. "So . . . Rome?" She looked around the ornate car. "It's nice," she told him, and he nodded.

"Yeah, it was this or the embassy in Tokyo—I told you that, right?"

Macey nodded. "Yeah. But I haven't talked to you since the move."

When the doors opened, I could tell we were on the top floor because the light was different. There was a tall window with a view of the city. Lush, thick carpet was beneath our feet.

"I'll just be a second," Preston whispered, pointing to the opposite end of the hall. "You guys can wait in the dining room. No one uses it in the morning. Cammie knows the way."

I started to say that, no, I didn't, but before I could utter a word, there was a man at the end of the hall, raising an arm and saying, "Cammie! You're here!"

The first time I ever saw Sam Winters, he was the governor of Vermont and a front-runner for the presidency of the United States. The last time I saw him . . . Well, judging by the way he threw open his arms and pulled me into a massive hug, it was pretty obvious I didn't remember the last time I'd seen him.

"How are you, Cammie? It's so good to see you and Preston back *together again*." Ambassador Winters lingered on the words, and from the corner of my eye, I saw Preston blush. "So, my dear, what brings you to Rome?"

"Fall break," I said, pleased with how natural the lie sounded. "And I knew I couldn't come to Italy without stopping by, because of . . ."

"Me," Macey said. "I insisted we come by even though it's early. We only have a few hours before we catch a connecting flight and leave town."

"Oh, Macey, dear. I didn't see you there." It was probably the first—and last—time that a man had missed seeing Macey McHenry, but no one said so. The ambassador was too busy giving Macey a hug and asking me, "And who are your friends?"

"Ambassador Winters, allow me to introduce my aunt Abby and her . . . boyfriend." Townsend tensed. Abby glared. And Rebecca Baxter looked like she was going to choke on her own chewing gum.

"And this is our roommate, Bex," Macey said.

Bex took the ambassador's hand and said hello in a way that would have made Madame Dabney extremely proud.

"And this is Zach," I said, rounding out the group; but Zach just stood stoically with his arms across his chest. (I guess the Culture and Assimilation curriculum at Blackthorne leaves a lot to be desired.)

"Welcome, welcome." Ambassador Winters gave a nod to the group, then turned back to me. "Now, I'm afraid I was just about to run out for a breakfast meeting at the Vatican, but I'm so glad you stopped by. Preston, take good care of these fine people."

"Yes, sir," Preston said.

His father slapped his hands together in the universal signal for *My work here is done*. But before he turned away, he reached for me, gave me one last hug. "Cammie, dear, it was good to see you again." He gave us one final smile. "You all come back any time."

And then he was gone, down the plush hallway as if he'd never been there at all.

Two minutes later, Preston was ushering us through a door and saying, "Can you wait in here a second?"

"This is fine, thanks," Abby told him, and then he was gone.

I looked around the room. There was a long table surrounded by a dozen high-backed chairs, all upholstered in the best Italian leather. Rich red curtains framed tall windows that overlooked the city. It was the kind of view that I'm pretty sure normal tourists would have remembered. But then again, I hadn't been normal in a very long time.

"So *you're* Zach." Townsend didn't even try to hide the judgment in his voice as he looked Zach up and down in some sort of silent but dangerous examination.

Zach huffed but smiled. "So *you're* Townsend."

The two of them stared for a long time, wordless. It felt a little like I was watching a documentary on the Nature Channel, something about alpha males in the wild. I didn't have a clue how it was going to end until Townsend nodded and took a deep breath.

"I suppose you should hear it from me that I have met your mother." He smiled a little sadly. "Well . . . when I say *met*, I mean one time I tried to kill her."

There was a charge in the air. Maybe it was the plush carpet beneath our feet, but I could have sworn I felt a spark.

"Do me a favor." Zach's voice was low and dark and dangerous. "Next time, don't just try."

Townsend smiled, and for a moment the two of them looked like long-lost friends.

"Boys," Bex said, dropping into the chair at the head of the table.

Abby rolled her eyes. "Exactly."

"Excuse me, Abigail, but whose shift did she get away during?" Townsend asked with a glare.

"Excuse me, Townsend, but who was supposed to booby-trap the doors?"

"I'm an agent of Her Majesty's Secret Service," Townsend said, indignant. "I do not do *booby* traps."

"Well, maybe you should start," Bex warned. "If you haven't heard, Cammie is pretty good at running away."

"I didn't run away," I snapped. Everyone stared. "I didn't. This time I sleepwalked away. And I came here."

"Why?" Abby asked me.

It was an excellent question—and lucky for me, that's when the one person in the world who might have been able to answer it opened the door at the rear of the room.

"So what brings you back to Rome, Cammie?" Preston said. He closed the door, and the smile slid from his face. "Why are you *really* here?"

If there was any way to lie, I could have done it. I had the training. The skills. But there comes a time—even for a Gallagher Girl—when the best weapon in your arsenal is the truth.

"Well, it's about last summer," I said slowly, and Preston turned to Macey.

"Do you know what this is about?" he asked, and Macey looked at Abby, who nodded *Go ahead*.

Macey opened her mouth, started to speak, but there's a feeling that comes when two halves of a girl's world collide. I could see it happening to Macey. The politician's son was meant to know her as the senator's daughter. He was never supposed to meet the Gallagher Girl.

It must have been harder than it sounds for Macey to look at him and say, "You know how I go to that boarding school? Well, it's—"

"A training academy for spies," Preston said as if it were the most obvious thing in the world. "I know," he said. "Cammie told me."

Then it was *my* turn to get the crazy glares.

"Indeed," Townsend said. He sounded like a man who had always suspected we Gallagher Girls must be easy to break.

"I had my reasons," I said. "I don't *remember* my reasons, but I'm sure I must have had them."

"When?" Abby asked, stepping toward Preston, hand on hip.

"Hey, I know you. You're the Secret Service agent who—"

"Got shot," Bex finished for him. "She got shot for Macey. She almost died for Macey. And now she's willing to die . . . *for her*." Bex pointed at me. "We're all willing to die for her. So answer the woman's question!"

"July." Preston looked afraid again. And he was right to. "She showed up on the Fourth of July. I remember because I'd been wishing there were fireworks." He looked at me. "Then you came and . . . well . . . I guess I got them."

"She came here—to this embassy—in July?" Abby asked.

"No." Preston shook his head. "She came to *me*."

The room was cold and still. Outside, the sun was beaming. It was going to be a gorgeous fall day, and I tried to imagine Rome in summer.

"You said you were backpacking through Europe and missed a train, got separated from your parents. That's what you said, at least."

"But you saw through me?" I asked, genuinely embarrassed.

"Really, Cam . . . you didn't even *have* a backpack." He laughed and shrugged. "At first I thought . . . well, I don't know what I thought. You were sick or something. You totally charmed Mom and Dad, though. They insisted you take the guest room across the hall from mine, and it felt like you slept for a week. You were so—"

"And you didn't call me!" Macey shouted. I saw Townsend shift, annoyed, but Macey couldn't be held back. "My friend shows up on your doorstep in a foreign country, exhausted and alone, and you didn't think 'Hey, maybe I should drop Macey a line'?"

"Macey," Abby said, but Macey pushed her aside.

"She was alone!" Six months' worth of worry and grief was pouring out of her. "She was sick and she was alone . . . all summer. She was alone," Macey said one final time and backed away.

Everyone—Bex and Abby, even Townsend and Zach—stood staring. It seemed to take forever for Preston to drop into a chair. "Do you ever think about Boston, Macey?" he asked. "About what happened on the roof? I do. I think about it all the time."

He ran his hands through his hair, then placed them on the table.

"I still dream about it sometimes." He made a slow circular motion in the air with one finger. "I see the helicopter—the way the shadow spun on the roof. I don't think I'll ever forget that spinning shadow. And the way the two of you didn't seem afraid. And that woman—" At the mention of his mother, Zach went horribly still. "I don't think I'll ever forget that woman." Preston shook his head and looked at Macey. "I think about it all the time."

"I know—"

"No," he snapped, cutting her off. "You don't. Because, if you did, then you'd know that when the girl who saved your life shows up on your doorstep hungry and exhausted, you take her in, and you bring her some food, and you wait for her to wake up. You want to know why I didn't call you? Because when that girl shows up on your doorstep, you do exactly what she says to do, and she said not to call *anyone*."

Preston pointed to me, then stood and paced to the windows that overlooked the front of the embassy where tourists and expatriates stood waiting for access to that small piece of American soil.

"Everyone comes here when they're lost."

It made sense, why I'd come there. The only question that remained was why I'd had to leave.

"Preston," I said, "was I . . . dangerous?"

"What?" he asked and shook his head. "You were sleepy. That's it. I thought you were just exhausted and needed a place to rest." He wheeled on me. "Now it's your turn to explain. What brings you back?"

"Preston, it's sort of . . . complicated. You know what happened on election night and in Boston, but you don't know about—"

"The Circle of Cavan," Preston filled in.

"Yeah, I—"

"Ms. Morgan," Townsend warned.

"It's okay," Preston told him. "These rooms are swept for bugs every day, and my dad doesn't allow regular surveillance in the family quarters. We can talk here." He looked at me. "You really don't remember?"

I shook my head. "No."

"Don't remember . . . what, specifically?" he asked.

I took a deep breath. "Summer."

I expected him to ask questions, to give me the Cammie's-lost-her-marbles or someone-is-playing-tricks-on-me looks, but they didn't come. Instead, he reached into his pockets and pulled out a passport and a small book bound in the Gallagher Academy's own library.

"I knew something was wrong," he said. "I thought you would call or something after you left, but—"

"She left?" Bex asked.

"Yeah. I came home one day and your stuff was gone. I found a stained towel and an empty box of hair dye . . . and these."

Zach reached for the passport and smiled. "I know this name. It's one of Joe's. You must have gotten it from his stash."

He handed the passport to Abby, but it was the book I was afraid to touch, not because it was unknown to me, but because I could recite every word and knew it had no place within those walls.

Bex turned to the first page and read the opening line: "'I suppose a lot of teenage girls feel invisible sometimes, like they just disappear . . .'"

"What is that?" Zach asked, and I shook my head. It felt so strange that he could know me and not know those words.

"It's a report," I said. "About what happened fall semester, sophomore year."

I'd written those words so long before, they felt almost like ancient history. I wasn't embarrassed, I realized, because in so many ways they had been written by another girl.

A silly girl.

A naive girl.

A girl who missed her father and longed for a normal life.

I didn't want normal anymore. Right then, I was willing to settle for life. Period.

"I brought a fake ID and an old CoveOps report to Rome. To sleep," I said, bewildered.

"No." Preston shook his head. "After a week or so you woke up and . . ." He trailed off, looked at us all in turn. "You were here, Cammie, because you said you needed to rob a bank."

Chapter twenty-six

The piazza was busy late the next afternoon. We stared down at it from the roof of a building across the way. I knew where the pigeons went when they scattered and what gelato stores were popular with tourists and which ones the locals preferred. But despite six hours of staring at la Banca dell'Impero, I still had no idea if I'd been there over my summer vacation. Or why.

All I really knew were the options.

Option one: forget what we'd heard and go back to school. Option two: call the CIA, the Marines, MI6, and the entire alumni association of the Gallagher Academy for Exceptional Young Women, and in the process, call a whole lot of attention to ourselves. Option three: we could watch and we could wait.

So option three was what we did.

"Guard change," Bex said, her eyes never moving from the binoculars that had been a permanent part of her face for hours. Townsend made a note, and I remembered the immortal advice of Joe Solomon that, at its heart, being a spy is boring. The older I got, the smarter my teachers became.

"Where's Zach?" I asked.

"Working," Townsend said from behind us.

"I want to work," I told him. "Why can't we work?"

"We are working, Cam," Bex reminded me. "Just . . . safely." Bex raised the binoculars again, and I thought about how neither she nor Macey had let me out of their sight all day. (I did, however, draw the line when Bex tried to handcuff herself to me before we napped that morning.)

It had been a full-time mission just staring down at the cobblestones, and I couldn't help but remember that this too would pass. I wasn't going to spend forever looking. Eventually, I had to get off that roof.

But I was still there an hour later when Zach and Preston climbed over the ladder that ran to the fire escape at the roof's edge.

"You got it?" Townsend asked.

"Yes, sir," Zach said, and I found it more than a little disturbing how fantastically the two of them were getting along. They were all monosyllables and perfect posture. I slumped against the stone railing, tired and annoyed.

"Don't mind me," I said. "I'm just the person who tried to rob the place last July."

"No, you didn't," Abby said, appearing on the roof. She was wearing a trim suit and tall black boots. Her hair was pulled into a sleek ponytail at the nape of her neck, and either I was imagining things or Townsend wasn't quite as good a spy as I thought, because I could have sworn I saw him drool a little.

Note to self: your aunt is a hottie.

"There was no break-in at that bank." The cool wind blew the ponytail, splaying dark tresses across Abby's fair skin, but she didn't move to brush the hair away as she turned to look at Townsend. "If Cammie, or well . . . Summer Cammie . . . came to Rome to visit that bank—"

"It was that one," Preston insisted, but Abby talked on.

"She either didn't do it—"

"Or she did it so well it didn't send up any flares?" Bex guessed.

Abby nodded. "Exactly." She turned to me. "So I don't think you did it."

"Maybe she did," Macey said, leaping to protect my honor. "Cammie could rob a bank."

"Yes, she could," Abby agreed.

I just sat there, craving gelato.

"But not that bank," Townsend said, stepping closer to my aunt and giving her a knowing nod.

The building across the way looked like a church or a beautiful old mansion. I'd been staring at it long enough to know it also looked like a fortress.

Preston inched forward, as if part of him knew that he'd stumbled (or been dragged) into a conversation that was about ten times beyond the clearance level of an ambassador's son.

"Like I told you yesterday and"—he looked at the group

and then at me—"*you* last summer, my dad banks there. That bank is popular with a lot of diplomats. Foreign dignitaries . . ."

"Spies," Aunt Abby finished for him.

"Your mom? Does your mom bank there?" I asked Zach, crossing the distance between us in three short strides. "Does she?"

He turned and stared into the distance. "I don't know. It seems like her sort of place." Then he turned back to me in a flash. "Which is why it's time to let the CIA take over." He cut his eyes at Townsend. "And MI6 if they want in."

"Oh," Townsend said slowly, "MI6 does."

"But—" I started, and Zach cut me off.

"But now we get you out of here." He reached for me.

"No," I said, jerking away.

I looked to my best friends for backup, but Bex just shook her head. "I agree with Zach."

"Big surprise," I huffed.

"You don't know what you're walking into, Cam," she told me. "You don't know why or how or even *if* you've walked in there before."

"I have to go," I told them all.

"No," Zach yelled. "You don't!"

"He's right, Ms. Morgan," Townsend said. "We've come this far. There are channels, operations—"

"The same channels that told the Circle they should send an assassin to stake out Joe Solomon's cabin?" I asked, but Townsend seemed indifferent to the point. "The last time we went through channels, I killed a man."

"The Circle could be here." Macey was beside me, pleading. "Did it ever occur to you that they have this place under surveillance just like the cabin was?"

"We've been staring down at that building for hours, Macey. Of course it occurred to me."

"But did you think about why there's no record of your having been there?" Bex said. "Did you think about—"

"What if *it's* still there?" I shouted. "I came to Rome for that—" I pointed to the bank. "I came looking for whatever is in there. . . . And what if it's *still* in there?"

"Ms. Morgan." Townsend sounded like the cold, calculating operative he was.

"Would you die to stop them, Agent Townsend?"

"Yes." He didn't miss a beat.

I pushed up my sleeves, revealing the fading slashes on my arms. "Then think about what I would do."

"Cam," Bex said, easing closer.

"You need me," I said, looking at Townsend and then Zach and Abby. "You never would have known about the embassy or Preston or the bank. You won't know what I know until I get inside." I breathed deeply. *"You need me."*

"Cam," Zach said. "You don't have to take this risk."

"Rome, Abby." I ignored him and turned to my aunt. "A month before my father disappeared, he needed you in Rome. Now *I* need you in Rome."

"I know." Abby's voice was small and fragile, and immediately I wanted to take the words back. But then she straightened and turned to the bank. "Where do we start?"

Chapter Twenty-Seven

Covert Operations Report

At approximately 0900 hours on Saturday, October 14, Operative Morgan was given a stern lecture by Agent Townsend, a tracking device by Agent Cameron, and a very scary look from Operative Goode. (She also got a tip that her bra strap was showing from Operative McHenry.)

The Operative then undertook a basic reconnaissance mission inside a potentially hostile location. (But it wasn't as hostile as Operative Baxter was going to be if everything didn't go according to plan.)

Walking across the square that morning, I should have been afraid. I looked down at my hands, waiting to see them shake a little, but they were steady; my pulse was even. I don't know if it was my training or my gut telling me that I was prepared—I was ready. But more likely it had something to do with the voices in my ear, talking over one another, giving orders all the way.

"Very good, Squirt," Aunt Abby said. "Now, stop at that corner and let us—"

"Keep walking, Ms. Morgan."

"Townsend," Abby snapped. "The southwest security camera is blinded."

"I've got eyes on her from the southwest," Zach said. "She's clear." I could see him on the far side of the piazza, reading a paper and staring through the morning crowds, looking right at me. "She looks great."

"Okay, Squirt, you know what to do," Abby said, and I walked on.

Agent Townsend was at my back, and Bex's voice was in my ear. "So far so good, Cam. Just keep walking." So I did. All the way across the square and through the bank's heavy doors, into a lobby that I could have sworn I'd never seen before.

The only thing that was familiar was the way Macey walked twenty feet in front of me in her tallest heels, her hand draped through Preston's arm. Every now and then she'd laugh and lean to rest her head on his shoulder. I wasn't entirely sure if it was a part of her cover or her natural tendency for really effective flirting (or, perhaps, her cover as a really effective flirt?), but the effect couldn't be denied.

No one in the lobby was looking at me.

"Okay, Cammie." Aunt Abby's voice was clear in my ear, and I heard her draw a deep breath. "What are you seeing?"

She didn't just sound like a CoveOps teacher—she sounded like *the* CoveOps teacher. So I took a casual turn around the floor and tried to do what Joe Solomon had been asking me to do for years: see everything.

There were fresh flowers on a table, and the ceilings were at least thirty feet high. The floors were made of stone and looked as old as the city itself. It was the kind of place that was built on wealth and prestige and the ability to keep the masses out. But whether or not I'd made it past those heavy doors before was something I couldn't say.

Across the room, Preston walked to one of the small tables and said, "I'd like to make a withdrawal, please." He pulled a wallet from his inner pocket and handed a card to the teller, while Macey leaned against him, smoothing the lapel of his jacket. She looked like a girl in love. Preston looked like a boy about to vomit all over a two-hundred-year-old table. And I kept turning, scanning the room as casually as I could.

"It's okay, Cam," Bex said in my ear. "You're just taking a look around. It's just a recon."

"Focus, Ms. Morgan," Townsend said.

"I am!" I hissed in his direction.

"Cam, think," Bex urged.

"It's . . ." I started, then shook my head in frustration. "Nothing." I felt like the least consequential person to ever grace that beautiful old building. "I've got nothing."

I'd never been more ashamed of my memory in my life.

"Okay," Abby said, "pull out. We'll regroup and—"

But then Abby's words didn't matter—*nothing* mattered besides the woman who was walking toward me, hand raised, saying, "*Signorina!* It's so good to see you again."

See you again...

For a moment I could have sworn I'd misunderstood—she must have been confused. But there was a smile of recognition on the woman's face as she leaned closer and gripped my hands and kissed me once on each cheek, saying, "*Ciao, ciao.*"

"Yes, yes," I said when finally her hands left mine. "It's so good to see you too."

"I told you, Roma is lovely in the autumn, is it not?"

"It is." I nodded, mirroring the woman's stance and expressions, trying my best to make Madame Dabney proud.

"You're here to see your box, no?"

Well, as a spy, needless to say, my first instinct was to lie. As a chameleon, what I really wanted to do was hide. But right then, more than anything, I was a girl who needed answers. So when the woman gestured to the stone staircase that spiraled down into the lower level and asked, "Shall we?" all I could think about were the words *your box*. And smile.

I had a box.

Across the lobby floor, I saw Townsend start my way, and Abby's voice was in my ear, saying, "Cammie, wait for Townsend. Wait for Townsend!"

But I'd already done enough waiting for a lifetime. I turned and followed the woman down the stairs, to a long hall with arched ceilings. The woman led me to a heavy door, too glossy and modern to really belong in that ancient building, and I knew that we were leaving the part of the bank the public got to see.

"Please," the woman said, gesturing to a small box beside the door.

"It's a retinal scan," I said.

"*Sì*," she told me with a smile.

Townsend had reached the bottom of the stairs and was heading our way. "We really should be—"

"There's a retinal scan," I told him. He seemed slightly taken aback, but not so much that the woman noticed.

"Sorry to keep you waiting," he said, staring right at me. "But we really should be leaving."

"And who might you be?" the woman asked, looking Townsend up and down.

"My guard," I told her.

"Of course," she said, unfazed. "As I explained to the *signorina* last summer, privacy and security are paramount. You are welcome to wait here, but once we are through these doors—"

"No," Townsend said just as, through my ear, Zach shouted, "Cammie, don't!"

But it was too late, because the heavy doors were already sliding aside, and I was already inside.

The woman kept talking about the weather and banking laws. She said something about liking my shoes and the changes to my hair. It was small talk. Never in my life have I been a fan of small talk—especially not when so many more pressing questions were flooding my mind.

Like, when had I been there, and why? Like, how did they have my retinal image, and where were we going? As we walked, I felt the floor sloping steadily downward. Gradually, the voices in my ears dissolved into static, and I was alone with the woman and the thick stone walls, on a path I totally didn't remember walking before.

As we turned a corner, I saw a man in a well-cut suit. The woman smiled at him, and he came forward.

"If the young lady will permit . . ." He reached for my hand and placed my forefinger into a small device that scanned my finger and pricked, pulling a tiny bit of blood.

"Ow!" I exclaimed, more out of shock than pain, and the man smiled as if he'd heard that before. Heck, he might have heard it from me.

Then the device beeped and another door swung open, and the man gestured me inside.

Number of minutes I waited: 20
Number of minutes it *felt* like I waited: 2,000,000
Number of times I wished I'd brought a book or something: 10
Number of tiles in the ceiling of that particular room: 49
Number of crazy scenarios that swirled through my head: 940

When the woman reappeared with a sleek metal case, she smiled and placed it on a small table, closed the door, and left me alone.

I knew it wasn't a bomb, of course, and yet, reaching for the lid, I could have sworn I felt my heart stop beating.

Had I purchased that safety deposit box when I was there last summer? Had I left a clue inside? Or was it just an elaborate cover, a ruse I'd used to access the bank and run some other scheme?

Those were just a few of the thoughts inside my head as I reached for the lid and slowly lifted, expecting anything but what I saw.

"Dad's journal?"

I'd wondered where it was for weeks, but holding it in my hands felt anticlimactic. "It's Dad's journal," I said again, just as there was a knock on the door.

"Is everything okay?" the woman asked.

"Yes," I called, shoving the journal into the back waistband of my jeans.

Looking down at the now-empty box, I tried to focus on the positive. "I was here," I told myself.

The fact should have made me happy. There was another point on the atlas, a thumbnail on the map of the war room in Sublevel One. But then I had to admit that the box itself was worthless. We had come a long, long way for nothing.

There was a new attendant waiting for me when I finally opened the door and stepped outside. He glanced behind me and saw the empty box sitting on the table, then asked in Italian if everything was okay.

"*Sì*," I told him. I started to turn and go back the way we'd come, but the man gestured in the opposite direction.

"This way," he said.

"But . . ." I pointed to where the main lobby lay.

"The exit is this way," he said, so I followed.

I don't know if it was some latent memory or just a sick feeling in my gut, but the comms unit in my ear crackled, and I felt alone with that strange man.

Way too alone.

The corridor slanted upward, and as we walked, I knew we had to be nearing the surface, and yet there was nothing but static in my ear.

Something was wrong, I knew it. And then the man leaned forward to push open a door. His blazer gapped, and that's when I saw the gun beneath his arm, holster unclasped and gun ready to draw.

A primal, urgent cry was sounding in my head, and before the sunlight even hit me, I was already spinning, kicking him to the ground, knocking his head against the stone wall and starting to run.

"I'm in an alley southwest of the bank," I said, but no one answered. Even the static was gone. I heard nothing but the revving of engines as two motorcycles started down the alley, coming fast.

I turned and bolted in the other direction. There wasn't a doubt in my mind that the bank had been compromised. My comms unit was silent. And the motorcycles were getting closer.

Soon they'd overtake me. My only hope was the street.

I had to make it to the street.

And then . . .

"Cammie!" a voice yelled. Ambassador Winters was parked in the mouth of the alley, throwing open the door of a car. "Get in!"

Chapter twenty-eight

It didn't feel like a rescue, and it wasn't an extraction. I studied Preston's father—the way he gripped the steering wheel too tightly and drove too fast down incredibly narrow cobblestone streets.

"Ambassador Winters, thank you so much. I was lost and—"

"Now's not the time for lies, Cammie," he said, glancing frantically at the street behind us. He hunched over the wheel in a totally inappropriate posture for high-speed driving as he examined the rearview mirror. "How many are there?"

"Excuse me?" I asked, dumbfounded.

"I know why you were at that bank, Cammie!" he snapped. "It's the same reason I helped you access it last summer. Now, how many men did the Circle send?"

"You're not an agent," I said. I could tell by the sweat beading at his brow, the death grip he kept on the wheel. He looked more like Grandpa Morgan than Joe Solomon. And yet the words were real: *the Circle*. "How do you know about—"

"I thought we covered this last summer, Cammie. Now, tell me how many—"

"One in the bank. Two on the street. Probably more along the perimeter."

He breathed deeply and spun the wheel, sending the black car skidding onto a narrow street that I doubt any tourist ever saw.

"How do you know about the Circle, Ambassador?"

He gave a short, nervous laugh. "I was almost President of the United States, Cammie. There are certain things that, at certain levels, you have to know. Not to mention that for a time, a lot of very smart people thought the Circle of Cavan was after my son." He glanced at me quickly from the corner of his eye. "I'm surprised you forgot that."

"I've been forgetting a lot lately."

I turned to the window as I said it. We were passing a bridge, and artists stood along the roadside with their canvases and paint. The skies were clear and blue. It was beautiful there.

But that was before the windshield shattered.

My head snapped, and the car spun.

I was faintly aware of the sensation of being weightless and then rolling, over and over. The crunching metal made a sickening sound. Shards of glass pierced my skin. It felt like I was running face-first through barbed wire. And yet all I could do was hope that I wouldn't be sick, knowing I would never recover from the shame of puking all over Preston's father.

When the car finally came to rest, the windshield was gone and the windows were shattered. There was nothing at all between me and the man who was climbing from his motorcycle and walking toward me—boots on cobblestones, broken glass crunching beneath his feet.

I shook my head and felt glass fall from my hair. Either it was luck or adrenaline, but I felt no pain or fear. Something in my training or my broken mind was taking over, and I was grabbing the ambassador's hand and pulling.

"Ambassador, we have to move. Do you hear me? We can't stay here."

The shrill sound of sirens echoed in the distance. A crowd was gathering. People called out in Italian that help was on the way. But from the corner of my eye, I saw two men crawling from the van that had struck us. A motorcycle revved in my ears, and I saw a second rider coming through the crowd.

"Ambassador, can you move?"

"What . . . Yes." He sounded groggy and disoriented—confused—so I gripped tighter.

"We have to run. Now."

A hundred yards away, I saw the entrance to the market we'd visited on our first day, with its stalls and merchants and tourists, and that was where I led, pulling as hard as I could, looking back over my shoulder at the men who followed us through the crowd. I tried to ignore the stares of the tourists, the blood running down the side of my face.

"Ambassador, stay with me," I said, talking as much about his mind as his body. "Do you have a panic button?"

"What?"

"Did your security detail give you a panic button? If so, press it *now*."

He shook his head. "Not since the campaign. What's that thing in your ear?" he asked. "Is it working?"

"No," I told him. "Someone's jamming the signal."

"So we're . . . alone?" he asked.

"Of course not," I said, trying to reassure him. "We're together."

The market seemed more crowded with the ambassador's arm around my shoulder, the two of us limping along side by side. Every few feet we had to stop for him to catch his breath or his balance.

"Cammie, you should go without me. Leave me here."

He had a point. Maybe he was in more danger with me than without me, but something told me that the men on our trail were the types who didn't like to leave any loose ends behind, and right then, Preston's dad wasn't a powerful dignitary. He was a witness.

"No luck," I told him, taking his hand. "You're stuck with me. Now, run."

"Where are we going?" he asked.

"The embassy." I thought about the walls, the gates, the marines. Rule of thumb: when in doubt, find a marine. "It's a quarter of a mile away."

"This is faster," he said, pointing to a secluded alley.

"No, Ambassador. We need crowds. Crowds are good," I

said. And I meant it; but that didn't mean it wasn't hard trying to slip between the crush of bodies, going against the current.

"There, Cammie." Mr. Winters pointed to a police officer walking our way.

"He's with them," I said.

"How do you—"

"Shoes," I whispered, and pulled Preston's dad behind a stall, slipping out of the fake officer's path. "He's wearing the wrong shoes."

"Oh . . ." The ambassador's voice was more like a whimper, and I hated myself for bringing my trouble to his doorway. "What did you mean, Cammie? When you said you were forgetting a lot lately?"

"I sort of have . . . amnesia." I spat out the word and shook my head. "I don't remember last summer."

"Just last summer?" he asked.

"Yeah. I know it sounds crazy and all but—"

"No." He wiped the sweat on his upper lip. Blood stained his sleeve. "Nothing really sounds crazy to me anymore."

I'd never thought about the things a person must see when they're a footstep away from the presidency. All good spies know that ignorance really is bliss. Mr. Winters looked like a man who knew things he truly wanted to forget.

I totally knew the feeling.

"Just a little bit farther," I told him when we left the market. The crowds were thinner on the broad, public street. I could see the embassy up ahead. "Ambassador?" I said, studying the blood that ran down his hairline. "Ambassador, stay with me. We're almost—"

But that was when I saw the van, big and white and coming far too fast. I should have run. I should have screamed. I should have done anything but stand there, locked in a memory of the year before, in Washington, D.C., as the Circle came for me the second time.

"Cammie," the ambassador said, shaking me. "Cammie, this way."

He was trying to pull me away from the van that had screeched to a halt in between us and the embassy. The door was sliding open. I wasn't sure where reality stopped and memory began. But it wasn't a grab team—not anymore. They didn't need me alive.

And then I heard the music, low and steady in the back of my mind. I started to sway. To hum.

To run.

"Open the gates!" I yelled, pulling the ambassador behind me.

A man was out of the van and coming closer, so I lowered my shoulder, rammed him as hard as I could, and never broke stride.

"Open the gates!" I yelled through the crowded street.

Everyone was turning, watching. The ambassador's arm was draped around my shoulders as I half pulled, half carried him toward the imposing building.

"The Ambassador," I yelled to the marines at the gates. "The Ambassador has been injured!"

I don't know whether it was my words or the sight of the man limping and bleeding, but the gates opened.

There were guards and marines, and a final, fading rev of a motorcycle engine as I dragged Preston's father past the fences, safely onto American soil.

Chapter twenty-nine

I kept the journal on my lap for the next five hours.

Townsend was behind the wheel of a car with tinted windows. Abby followed us on a motorcycle, looping in front for a while, then falling behind, a constant circle of surveillance. Zach and Bex were in the tail car, and I only registered enough to be grateful that Zach was driving (a person can't go through Driver's Ed with Rebecca Baxter without being at least a little bit traumatized by the experience).

But I didn't ask where the cars came from.

I didn't wonder where we were going.

I didn't mention the men who had chased me from the bank.

To do that would have meant 1) wondering if I'd walked into that very trap last July; and 2) admitting that we'd gone to all that trouble to get a journal that I'd had six months before.

Summer, it seemed, had happened for nothing.

"Cam?" Macey's voice was soft. The car stopped. "Cam," she said, and I felt a touch on my shoulder, a light shake. "We're here."

Here, it turned out, was another safe house, this one an abandoned villa on a small lake north of Rome.

"We'll rest tonight," Townsend said from the driver's seat while Zach pulled open my door.

"Come on, Gallagher Girl," he said. "Try to get some sleep."

I took his hand and stepped from the car. We were far enough north that the air was significantly cooler, and the breeze felt like a slap, waking me from my daze.

"I don't need sleep, Zach. I need answers."

"Cammie, we already know so much," Bex said, and I wheeled on her.

"We don't know anything. We don't *have* anything except *this*." I held up my father's journal. "Which, by the way, we had last semester. We don't know where I went or what they did to me." I heard my voice crack. "We don't know where I messed up."

Suddenly, it all became too much, so I took the journal I treasured above everything else and hurled it against the car.

"Cammie!" Abby sank to her knees on the dusty driveway, and I don't know what was more surprising, the shocked pain of my aunt's expression or the small envelope that leaped from between the pages and fluttered to the ground at her feet.

"What is it?" Bex asked, reaching for the letter that must

have been tucked inside the book I hadn't even bothered to open. "Is it from you, Cam?"

"No," I said, shaking my head and looking at my father's handwriting—at the words *For my girls*. "It's *for* me."

There was cheese and stale bread in the kitchen. Macey scavenged for bottles of olives and a few mismatched plates, while Zach built a fire and Townsend and Bex checked our perimeter. But Abby and I just sat staring at the letter that lay in the center of the old kitchen table, like it was too precious or dangerous to touch.

I'd seen my father's handwriting before, of course. I'd read his entire journal, memorized every word. But something about that letter felt different, as if he were calling to me from beyond the grave.

After a while, the others took their seats at the table, but no one reached for the food. We just sat, watching, until the silence became too much.

"Read it," I told Aunt Abby, pushing the letter toward her; but she shook her head no.

"We'll take it to Rachel. She can—"

I pulled the envelope away and handed it to Bex. "You do it."

"Cam . . ."

"I need to know," I said, and she didn't argue. She just picked it up and started to read.

"'Dear Rachel and Cammie, If you are reading this, then I

am probably gone. Well, that or Joe finally found the hole in his cabin wall where I've been stashing things for years. Or both. In all likelihood, it's both.'"

I know Bex's voice almost better than I know my own, but as she spoke, the words shifted and faded. I heard my father as my best friend read.

"'Please forgive me for not giving this to you myself, but as long as there's a chance that I can go on without putting anyone else in danger, I have to take it. I think that I have the key—quite literally—to bringing the Circle down. But a key does no good without a lock, and that's the next thing I have to find. I've stored the key in a bank box in Rome that only you and Cammie and I will be allowed to access.'"

"Rome," Abby whispered. Guilt and grief filled her eyes, but there was no time to think about it, because Bex kept reading aloud.

"'I shouldn't say any more here, in case this note falls into the wrong hands, but once you have the key, you will understand. If I am right, then there is a way to bring the Circle to an end, a window that can lead to a happy ending. And I will find it. I promise you I will.

"'I love you both.'" Bex laid the letter on the table, and I stared numbly at the words until my gaze came to rest on the three letters at the bottom of the page.

M.A.M.

Matthew Andrew Morgan.

"Cam," Bex was saying. "It will be okay. We will—"

"I . . . I saw this."

"Yeah, Cam," Macey said. "You had the letter. You found it at Joe's cabin and took it to Rome and—"

"Not in Rome." My hands shook as they traced my father's initials. The paper was smooth, but what I felt was rough stone and crumbling mortar.

"Cammie," Abby said softly. "Cam!" she snapped, pulling me back.

"Aunt Abby." I heard my voice crack. "We need to get the car."

Chapter tHiRty

My memory wasn't back. It wasn't as simple as that. But there were flashes—images and sounds. I felt my head spinning like a compass, guiding us for hours until our ears popped and the snow blew, and I stared out our car window, looking for anything that seemed familiar.

No one spoke as the roads grew narrower, steeper. I didn't know if it was the altitude or the situation, but I found it harder and harder to breathe until I said "Turn here" for reasons I didn't quite know.

We drove on. The road turned to lane and then . . . to nothing. Agent Townsend stopped the SUV. "It's a dead end," he said, and Abby turned to me.

"It looks different in the winter, Squirt. Don't pressure yourself or—"

"I've been here." It wasn't just the feeling of waking up in the convent, the memory of the chopper ride down the mountain. I knew that air. "We're close," I said, and before anyone could stop me, I reached for the door and was out, wading through the drifts.

The flashes were stronger then, clearer than they had been on the hillside with Dr. Steve. Those rocks were the same rocks. The trees were the same trees. And when I saw the broken branches, I knew that I had broken them on purpose—that I'd known someone would come looking for me eventually and I wanted to show them the way.

I just hadn't known that that someone would be me.

"Are you sure?" Bex said from behind me. "Are you positive that this—"

I reached out for a piece of pine, my blood still on the bark. "This is the place."

It took an hour to reach it—the ruins of an old stone house that stood alone, crumbling at the top of the mountain.

"I was here," I said.

The images in my mind were black-and-white and blurry, but I felt it in my bones. My dreams were coming back, but they weren't dreams. And yet they weren't quite memories either as I pushed through a creaking wooden door and walked through rooms I didn't recognize, listened to sounds I didn't know. Only the feel of the stones beneath my fingers was familiar.

There was a cold fireplace filled with black logs and forgotten ashes. It hadn't burned in months, but I heard the crackle of the fire.

Two bowls sat on a table, cold to the touch, but I could taste the food.

I'd already broken free once, but there was something in that building that hadn't let me go.

Townsend and Abby were wordless, efficient. Opening drawers, scanning floorboards. They covered every inch of the old stone house until they finally huddled together and spoke in low, conspiratorial whispers.

"Nothing," Abby told him. "You?"

"This place is clean," he said.

But I just turned to the small door that led to the narrow cellar stairs, and said, "Down there."

Zach was at my back, following me into the musty cellar. There was one tiny window high on the wall, barely peeking over the ground.

"Come on, Gallagher Girl," he said. "Don't do this to yourself. The Circle never leaves anything behind." My fingers traced the walls beside a narrow bed. "They never use a safe house twice."

And then my fingers found the letters scratched into the mortar between the stones.

C.A.M.

Cameron Ann Morgan

My hand began to shake as it pushed the mattress aside, revealing three more letters hidden below.

M.A.M.

Matthew Andrew Morgan

"Yes," I told Zach, my voice flat and cold and even. "They do."

* * *

Zach couldn't hold me in the room. Agent Townsend couldn't stop me on the stairs. I was too strong in that moment. I wasn't running from that place or its ghosts. I was running to something, for something, as I burst through the door and out into the snow.

The woods were alive with flashes and beats, images that came in black-and-white, like I'd seen it all before in a dream. But not a dream, I realized. A nightmare.

Bring the girl, a voice said.

Show her what happens to spies who don't talk.

My mind didn't know where I was going, but my legs did. They took me over banks and around pine trees. My body was impervious to the cold and the boy at my back yelling, "Cammie!"

Zach was struggling to keep pace behind me, but all I heard was the music, and the cold voice saying, *The least we can do is take her to her father.*

I skidded to a stop at the edge of the trees, exhaling foggy, ragged breaths, staring into the small clearing. But it wasn't a clearing—I knew it. The outline of the trees was too precise, the corners too square to be random.

Snow covered the ground, and yet I knew that patch of earth. I'd felt it calling to me for weeks, pulling me back to that mountain.

"It's real," I said.

Abby was behind me, panting from the altitude. Zach tried to put his arms around me. He didn't know my shaking had nothing to do with the cold.

When I began to say, "No. No. No," he didn't know I was revolting against, not a memory, but a fact.

"What is this?" Townsend was there finally, Bex at his side.

But it was Macey who stood apart from the others, seeing the small clearing at a distance. And that's why she was the first to realize, "It's a grave."

"No. No." I fell to my knees and began to scrape blindly through the white.

"Cammie." Townsend's hands were on mine, but Abby was already on her knees beside me, scraping too.

"Cammie!" Zach yelled, and pulled me to my feet and into his arms. "Stop."

"He's there," I said, the words blending into sobs. "He's there. He's there."

Abby didn't scream, but she kept clawing, her bare hands bleeding in the snow.

"It's over." Agent Townsend reached for her. He didn't scold or scoff. He just smoothed her hair, pressed his cheek against hers, and said, "He's gone."

Chapter thirty-one

I know the theories behind interrogation tactics. I've seen the tutorials. I've read all the books. In the part of my mind that was still thinking, processing, planning, I knew that if the Circle had wanted to break me, there was no better place than my father's grave to do it. I stared at my reflection in the window of the car that carried us back to school twelve hours later—at my sunken eyes and thin frame—and I thought about the nightmares and the sleepwalking.

I knew it might have worked.

When the school gates parted, I couldn't help but remember the first time I'd ever set foot behind those walls. It was the August after my father disappeared, and I had spent every day since wondering where he had gone and what had happened. For years I'd thought that not knowing was the hard part. But right then all I wanted to do was forget.

When the car finally stopped, I watched my friends climb from the backseat of the limo, saw Townsend take Abby's hand, hold it tightly in his own and say, "If you'd like, I can come inside and help. . . ."

"No." Abby shook her head. "I'll tell her."

Mom, I thought, the cold realization sweeping over me. Someone was going to have to tell Mom. And right then I was certain that Summer Me must have been willing to trade her memory for not having to face that moment.

I knew because it was a trade I would have willingly made again.

"Ms. Morgan." Agent Townsend's hand was on my shoulder, squeezing twice. He didn't say anything else. He didn't have to. Then he climbed back into the limo, and I stayed frozen, watching him drive away.

"Cam, come on," Macey said, but I just stood there looking up at the moon. It was the first time in years I didn't wonder if my father was out there, looking at it too.

"Cammie!" someone yelled, and something in Bex's face made me turn to look at Liz, who stood in the doorway, light streaming around her yellow hair. She looked almost like an angel, and I expected her to say, "I heard about your dad."

I thought she might scream, "I'm so sorry."

Liz is the kindest of us all. I fully expected her to throw her arms around me and let me cry and cry until I couldn't cry anymore.

What I wasn't prepared for was to see her smile.

And yell, "It's Mr. Solomon! Mr. Solomon is awake!"

* * *

Liz's hand was in mine. She was running up the stairs, pulling me along. And while I know that, physically, Liz really isn't a match for any of us, right then I couldn't stop her. As soon as we reached Joe Solomon's secret room, though, I froze, unable to go inside.

"Mr. Solomon!" Bex yelled, pushing past me, Macey on her heels. Then Aunt Abby was beside me, her hand on my shoulder, but neither of us moved. We just stood there staring at the woman by the bed.

She didn't look like a spy or a headmistress or even a mother in that moment. She was just a woman. And she was beaming.

"Hi, girls," Mom said. She held his hands and smiled at me. "Look who's up."

I don't think I realized it at the time, but a part of me had been wondering if I'd ever see my mother happy again. A part of me was wondering if *I'd* ever be happy again. But the look on my mother's face was one of pure, undeniable joy. I turned to my aunt, saw that realization in her eyes too, and then, more than ever, I wanted to run away and take my bad news with me.

"Welcome back, ladies," Mr. Solomon said, but his voice sounded different, as if the smoke from the tombs was still in his lungs.

He was propped a little higher than he had been when he was sleeping. A little color filled his cheeks, but his lips were chapped and dry. Mom held a cup to his mouth, and he sipped, then smiled at her, but the effort must have been too much for him, because he started coughing.

I'd slept for six days. Joe Solomon had been out for six months. I didn't want to know what that felt like.

"Joe!" Zach cried, pushing past me and Bex and Macey, rushing to his mentor's side. "Joe . . ." He let the word trail off.

"Well, Rachel, the standards in this place must be dropping. I go to sleep and they start letting just anyone in here," Mr. Solomon said, then coughed again. And I realized just how much tension there must have been in the room for a man like him to try to break it.

"Cam, Abby, *Joe's awake*," Mom said, because I guess our expressions weren't at all what she was expecting. "Isn't that wonderful?"

"Yes. Of course," Abby said. Faint traces of dirt and blood still clung to her fingers. Her voice cracked when she said, "We missed you so much."

Only Liz seemed to share my mother's smile as she studied the machines. "The brain scans and EEGs are really good." She spoke to us all, but she looked at Mr. Solomon. "You look really good."

"Thank you, Ms. Sutton."

"You do," Mom said, leaning closer to my teacher. "You look perfect."

Zach was smiling like I'd never seen him smile before, looking down at the closest thing to family he had left. But not me. I was thinking that I would never get to smile at my father again.

"So," Mr. Solomon said, "what did I miss?"

A lot of people think that being a Gallagher Girl means

not being afraid of anything. Actually, that couldn't be further from the truth. It's not about ignoring fear. It's about facing it, knowing the risks and the costs and sacrificing safety and security anyway. I'd seen my aunt Abby jump in front of a bullet once, and yet in that moment she was terrified. I didn't want to know what I looked like.

"What is it?" my mother said, but I was already turning from the room that held so many people who didn't know that this wasn't the time to be happy.

"Rachel." I heard my aunt's voice fading away. "We need to talk."

Of all the nooks and crannies, the narrow passageways and grand halls that comprise the Gallagher Academy for Exceptional Young Women, my very favorite space might possibly be the Protection and Enforcement barn at night. The moon shines through the skylights, and in the dark it's all stillness and shadows. Plus, it's the only place on campus where it's almost always okay to hit things.

"You're making a bad habit out of this."

I don't know what was more surprising—that Zach had found me so quickly or that he'd actually left Joe's side. If the man I loved like a father were upstairs, I don't think I'd walk away from him ever again.

"You should be with him," I said, standing at the center of the mats, looking up at the moon.

Zach stepped closer. "I'm right where I need to be."

"Did Abby . . ."

"She's telling them now."

"Is Joe your father, Zach?"

I don't know where the question came from, but it was out, and I couldn't take it back even if I'd wanted to.

"No." Zach shook his head. "I never knew my dad. I don't know anything about him."

Suddenly I felt guilty for my foolishness. For my crying and my tantrums. After all, nothing could have made me trade mourning my father for not knowing him.

"I'm sorry," I said.

"I'm not. I have Joe."

"I'm glad he's awake," I said. My throat burned. "I'm glad he's . . . back."

"Gallagher Girl," Zach said, reaching for me, but I stepped away.

"My dad's not coming back," I said.

"I know."

"He's not missing, Zach. He's dead."

"I know."

"They killed him!"

"You're alive, Cammie."

"Mr. Solomon is alive," I said, and Zach took my arms and squeezed them tight.

"*You're* alive."

"My dad . . ."

"*You're alive.*"

I don't know how long I cried. I don't know when I slept. All I know is that Zach's arms were still around me when I woke on the mats, lying in the center of the floor.

"Go back to sleep," he said, smoothing my hair.

I'd been sleeping. I realized that I'd been sleeping and I hadn't dreamed.

"Zach," I said as I lay there. "Where did you go? When you were looking for me?"

I shifted in his arms, looked into his eyes.

"Crazy." His voice was a whisper against my skin. "I went crazy."

Chapter Thirty-two

Things That Simply Must Be Done When
You Miss Three Days of School, Survive a
Terrorist Attack, Visit the Place You Were
Tortured, and Solve the Mystery That Had
Pretty Much Dominated Your Entire Life
(A list by Cameron Morgan)

- Laundry. Sure, it's not the most exciting part of
  post-op life, but it's a part of it nonetheless.

- Homework. It is either a great advantage OR
  disadvantage to have Elizabeth Sutton in charge of
  collecting class notes and assignments while you're
  gone. Really, it's a toss-up.

- Paperwork. Because even unauthorized missions
  have A LOT of people who have to be kept in the
  loop. Eventually.

- Answer the well-meaning but slightly nosy questions of well-meaning but slightly nosy classmates (delegated to Rebecca Baxter).

- Figure out how to make it look like you haven't spent the past few days crying (or trying not to cry) (delegated to Macey McHenry).

- Do your best to get on with your life.

———

For reasons that had nothing to do with my mother's cooking ability (or lack thereof), I totally wasn't looking forward to Sunday night.

Sure, we have a lot of traditions at the Gallagher Academy, and Sunday night dinners alone with my mom in her office were usually one of my favorites. I didn't wear my uniform. She didn't talk about the school. We weren't headmistress and student on those nights. We were mother and daughter. And that was why I stood in the Hall of History for a long time, almost afraid to knock.

The door was open just a crack, and I could see my mom inside, sitting on the leather sofa, her legs curled up beneath her as she fingered the gold ring on her left hand. She turned it over and over, then pulled it from her finger, held it up to the light as if looking for some kind of crack or flaw.

My father had been dead for years, but my mother had only been a widow for a week, and suddenly I felt guilty for standing there, spying. I wanted to slip away, but when I moved, the floor squeaked and my mom yelled, "Cammie?"

"Yeah," I said, easing the door open. "Sorry to bother you. I just . . ."

I stepped inside.

"It's Sunday," Mom said. Her expression changed as she realized what day it was—what that day meant. "I'm so sorry, sweetheart. I forgot all about—"

"That's okay. I've got a lot of homework to make up anyway. I'll just go."

"No. Sit. Stay. I can call the kitchen and order some . . ." She trailed off.

"I'm not hungry," I said.

"Okay. Then we'll just talk." She sat up straighter and patted the seat beside her. "So, kiddo, how are you?"

"Fine," I said, and I tried to mean it. I really, really did. "How is Mr. Solomon?"

"Better," Mom said. "The news . . . it set him back a little."

I nodded because, let's face it, I totally knew the feeling.

"What do you . . . I mean, what do we tell Grandma and Grandpa?"

Mom's hand stroked my hair. Her voice was soft and low. "There's nothing we can tell them, sweetheart. As far as your grandparents know, their son is already buried in the family plot in Nebraska. To tell them any different now . . ."

"Of course. Yeah," I said, shaking my head. "They shouldn't have to go through this. They should get to stay . . . at peace."

"I agree." Mom nodded. She smiled. Peace seemed like the

operative word. When I looked at her, I knew I wasn't the only one who had been searching, running. Everything was different now that my father was officially "in from the cold."

"Joe and I have been talking. We think maybe in a few months, when he's stronger, we might have another service—something small. Would you like that?"

Would I like to bury my father? Again? I sighed when I realized the answer. "Yes."

"And there will be a ceremony at Langley. They're keeping his remains there for now, and we can go up when the semester's over if you'd like."

"Sure," I said. "Okay." I didn't want to talk about it anymore—none of it. I'd already done enough talking with Dr. Steve.

"What is it, Cammie? What's bothering you?"

It seemed like a ridiculous question, and I wanted to snap at her, ask her where she wanted me to begin. But when I opened my mouth, the only words that came out were "I lost the key."

Okay, I don't know what I had expected to say, but that totally wasn't it. And yet, there it was—the one thing I hadn't had the strength to say to anyone. Not to my roommates. Not in my sessions with Dr. Steve. And not to Zach.

It was my father's final mission—the very last thing he'd asked me to do, and I'd failed. So I searched my mother's eyes and told her the thing that hurt the most right then.

"In Dad's letter, he said there was a key. Summer Me must

have gotten it out of the box, and now it's gone. He left that for us. . . . He might have died because of it, and I—"

"Cammie, no. Do you hear me, no." My mother sounded angry and scared. She reached for my shoulders and turned me to face her. "Do not worry about this. Your father's legacy was not some key. Your father's legacy has not been locked up in a Roman bank vault for the past five years—it's been here. On this couch. With me."

Her grip tightened.

"*You* are your father's legacy. And all he would care about—all *I* care about—is that we still have you."

Tears filled her eyes, but she didn't move to wipe them away. "Do you know that?"

I nodded, unable to speak.

"Okay."

Neither of us spoke again for a long time. It was a sound I was used to. When you grow up in a house full of spies, you grow accustomed to silence. Life is classified. There is always so much that goes unsaid.

"That week—before he left—he took me to the circus, did I ever tell you that?"

"Well"—Mom laughed—"you both spent the next couple of weeks eating leftover cotton candy, so, yes, I knew. For an excellent spy, he was a terrible sneaker."

"He seemed so happy."

"He was happy, sweetheart. He loved you so much."

"That was a good day," I said, curling up beside my mother.

"There were a lot of good days," she said, and I knew that it was true. I closed my eyes, felt my mother stroke my hair, and the music was softer then, in the very back of my mind as I drifted off to sleep, knowing my mother was with me.

There were still good days to come.

Chapter THIRTY-THREE

It wasn't until Friday morning that I noticed the book that Liz was carrying, reading under her desk while Madame Dabney lectured at the front of the room.

"What are you doing with that?" I asked, pointing to the bundled pages.

"It's the CoveOps report you wrote after the whole Josh thing sophomore year," she whispered. "The one Summer You took to Rome."

"I know," I said, pulling the book from her hands. "What are you *doing* with it?"

"Reading," Liz hissed and pulled the book back.

"You've already read it," I told her.

"I know."

"That means you've already *memorized* it," I reminded her, and Liz rolled her eyes.

"Re-reading can be very beneficial."

I looked at Bex, who was sitting on Liz's other side. She raised her eyebrows, and I knew what she was thinking. I'd carried that book to Europe. Of all the tools and devices, resources and gear, I'd taken *that*. Summer Me might have been on the run, but she wasn't a fool.

Walking out of class that day, I found myself staring at the entrance to the secret passageway that led to Mr. Solomon's room.

"You should go see him, Cam," Zach said, appearing beside me.

"I don't know what to say," I admitted.

"He was your dad's best friend," Bex said. "He understands."

"That's not it," I had to say.

Bex crossed her arms and leaned against the wall, blocking my path until I said, "I ran away, Bex. And I got caught." The plain truth settled down on me. "Joe Solomon wouldn't have gotten caught."

It felt as though a wave of seventh graders were washing over us—a tide made of tiny rain-soaked uniforms and backpacks heavier than the girls who wore them. I smashed myself against the wall, huddled with my roommates and Zach, and watched them pass.

"Were we ever that short?" I asked.

Bex looked at me. "You were. I wasn't."

"We're seniors," I said. Even without the massive memory loss, it seemed like we'd reached that point too quickly.

"When did everything get so . . . complicated?" Liz wanted to know, and suddenly it sounded like a very good question.

"That's it!" I blurted. "When *did* everything get complicated?"

"Boston," Macey said with a shrug.

"No." Zach shook his head. "I started hearing chatter earlier—that summer. Why?"

"I used to wonder why the Circle wanted me," I said. "But maybe that was the wrong question. Maybe what I should have been asking was why does the Circle want me *now*?"

"What does that matter?" Zach asked.

"My dad disa— My dad died." I forced myself to say it, choking on the word. "He died when I was in the sixth grade, but they didn't come after me until last year. Why wait until I'm a junior in spy school? Why wait until I can fight back?"

"So either they didn't need you then . . ." Liz started.

"Or they didn't *know* they needed you," Macey finished.

"Something changed." I nodded, unable to shake the feeling that there was something we were missing—that there was something that the girl I'd been in June had already known. "So what was it?"

"Well . . ." Macey rolled her eyes and started down the rapidly emptying hall. "You discovered boys."

She started to laugh at the joke, but Liz was already tearing open her backpack. "The CoveOps report! Cam, they came for you after you wrote this!" We all looked down at the book. "Summer You must have known that, so you took the report to re-read it and try to figure out what or why or . . . what."

"Liz, I don't know," Macey said, turning back. "It was just boy stuff. I mean, Cam was goo-goo for Josh and all, but he wasn't exactly international-incident-worthy." I saw Zach tense a little, but no one acknowledged his discomfort. "What does the Circle of Cavan care about Cam's first boyfriend?"

"I don't know, Macey." In the back of my mind, I heard the music, lower than before. "But Liz is right. I wrote that over Christmas break. It went through channels that spring. And then a few months later, Zach heard that there was a Gallagher Girl the Circle was after. Now, maybe it's a coincidence but . . ."

"Maybe it's not." Zach's voice was cold.

Bex nodded. "Maybe there are no coincidences."

If there was ever any doubt that Joe Solomon was a better operative than I was, it totally went away that Saturday evening.

"Hello, Ms. Morgan."

The voice came to me from the dark shadows of my suite, and, spy skills or not, I totally jumped. (And I might have squealed a little too.)

The light flickered on, and there he was, sitting in the chair next to Liz's desk. There were no crutches, no cane—just one of the world's greatest living spies . . . living.

"You're . . . up?"

I didn't know what was more troubling, that recently-out-of-a-coma Joe Solomon could sneak up on me, or that supposed-to-be-dead Joe Solomon was out roaming the halls on his own.

"Where are your roommates?"

"I . . ." I glanced around the suite as if to make sure they weren't there too. "I don't know," I said as evenly as I could with Mr. Solomon sitting there like a ghost.

"That's okay, Cammie," Mr. Solomon said. "It's you I really wanted to see. So, how was your day?"

"Fine, I guess," I said, because Saturdays were always crazy—between P&E and makeup tests, Dr. Steve's therapy sessions and general weekend*ness*, they always flew by in a blur.

"Good." His voice had grown clearer. Stronger. He sounded almost like himself. "It's good to see you, Cammie."

"It's good to see you too. How . . . are you?"

"I'll be fine," he said.

"How are you *now*?" I asked, stronger this time, and my teacher smiled, proud of me for recognizing that he hadn't actually answered my question.

"I'm better," he said. "I like the short hair."

I brought my hand up and touched the ends. To tell you the truth, I'd almost forgotten it had changed. I guess I'd gotten used to it. I wondered what else I would eventually forget to miss.

"He's really gone, isn't he, Mr. Solomon?" I said, staring at the books on Liz's desk. I couldn't meet his eyes when I whispered, "My dad is really dead."

"I know, Cammie." Mr. Solomon didn't sound like he'd been crying. He didn't sound any different at all, and he must have read my eyes, because he hurried to add, "I have always known."

"How?"

"Because death is the only thing that could have ever kept him from you."

I didn't want to think about my father. Not his life. Not his death. And most of all, not about the mission that had killed him—the mission that I had tried, and failed, to follow. I'd spent years on that path, searching for the truth. But I didn't want the truth, I realized. What I wanted was my dad. And all that was left was a cold trail and an empty box.

I reached up and touched the necklace that hung around my neck, my hands eager for something to do.

"I should get you back downstairs," I told my teacher. "You're going to need your rest and—"

"Cammie—" Mr. Solomon was easing slowly toward me, his voice calm and strong and even. *"Cammie, where did you get that necklace?"*

Chapter THIRTY-fOUR

When an operative (not to mention teacher) like Joe Solomon tells you to do something, you do it. Even if it goes against doctor's orders. Even if it doesn't really make any sense. Even if you can't find a wheelchair and he's still in his flannel PJs.

When Joe Solomon grips your hand and says, "Professor Buckingham. Take me to her. Now," you go.

I knew that Dr. Fibs had developed some new technology that would keep Mr. Solomon's muscles from atrophying during his long sleep, but he'd been in that bed for months, and it was all I could do to help him start down the hall and into one of the passageways that would keep us hidden from the other students. I tried to tell him that I could go get help, but Joe Solomon was one of the best operatives in the world. He wasn't going to be delayed one second more, so he leaned against me and we made our way downstairs.

"Don't worry, Mr. Solomon. Mom's probably in her office. We can—"

"Not your mom. Patricia," he said, breathing hard.

"Professor Buckingham?" I asked. It didn't make any sense, but Mr. Solomon just nodded and I kept walking.

It was harder than it should have been to feel Joe Solomon leaning against me. It wasn't the weight. It was that the strongest man I knew seemed helpless. And I didn't like it at all, but I kept going, climbing down stairs and finally into the main hallway on the second floor. I peeked out to make sure it was empty, then helped Mr. Solomon out behind me. We were almost there when—

"Cameron Morgan!" I heard Buckingham exclaim from behind us. "What is the meaning of this?" She looked around and pulled us into a quiet alcove, lest any nosy eighth graders passed by and saw me walking the halls with Joe Solomon's ghost.

"Now, you wait here," she ordered. "I will get some help and we will get you back to your room."

"The necklace, Cammie. Show her the necklace."

I'm not exactly proud of it, but I actually worried that Mr. Solomon might be seeing things, thinking things—that maybe I had lost my memory and he had lost his mind. But I reached up and found the chain that hung around my neck just the same. I ran my hands along it until I found the small medallion.

"Take that off," Buckingham ordered, so I gave it to her. She stepped out of the shadows and held the small charm against the light.

"Joe, is that . . ." she started.

"I think so, Patricia. I think . . ." But then he faltered and stumbled into my arms. "I need to sit down."

Five minutes later, we were all settled into Mom's office with my roommates and Zach and Abby, and Mom was saying, "What is it?"

"Your necklace, Cammie," Buckingham said. "Show it to them."

"I don't understand what the big deal is," I said, taking it off again and holding it forward. "It's nothing, Mr. Solomon. Tell him, Mom," I said, looking at her. "I was in Rome last summer, and I bought a bunch of jewelry for everyone. Souvenirs and stuff."

"Look at it, Cammie," Mr. Solomon said, and I couldn't help myself: I smiled because he sounded . . . like Mr. Solomon. I could tell Bex had heard it too.

"Cammie," Mr. Solomon warned, and I did as I was told.

There was a small silver charm on a matching chain. The charm looked like a shield divided into two, with a large tree covering the center, its branches touching both sides. "What do you see, Ms. Morgan?" my CoveOps teacher asked.

"It's a seal of some kind. Probably something to do with Rome—that's where I bought it and—"

"No one bought that necklace, Cameron," Buckingham told me.

"Yes, I did," I countered.

Mr. Solomon cocked his head. "I thought you didn't remember?"

"Well, technically, I don't. But we know I got a bunch of jewelry at the street fair in Rome."

"You got it in Rome, I'm sure. But you didn't buy it." He straightened on the couch. "I strongly suspect you retrieved that necklace from your father's safety deposit box," Mr. Solomon said, and suddenly it didn't feel like a five-dollar trinket I'd picked up at the fair. It felt priceless. And that was before my teacher talked on.

"What do you see when you look at it?" he asked.

"I don't remember, Mr. Solomon. I've tried, I swear. I just don't—"

"Not what do you *remember*. What do you *see*?"

"It's a crest," I said. "It kind of reminds me of the Gallagher Academy seal but without the sword and stuff. I thought that was why I bought it."

"It's not *like* the Gallagher *Academy* seal, dear," Buckingham said. "It *is* the Gallagher *family* seal."

My mom was shaking her head. "I didn't know. I've never seen that." She turned to her sister. "Abby?"

"Me either," Abby said. "How is that possible?"

"Oh, very few people alive today would recognize it," Buckingham told them. "Gillian took great pains to remove all traces of her family seal when she inherited the mansion. I'm not surprised you didn't know what that emblem was."

Everyone was slowly creeping closer to me. I felt them closing in as the crest lay in the palm of my outstretched hand.

"Why did Matthew have it, Joe?" Abby asked.

Mr. Solomon laughed and shook his head. "I didn't know he did. Matt was . . . stubborn."

Mom sat at her desk, not moving. I didn't want to look at her, but her presence was like a fire burning at the corner of my eye.

"There was a lot he didn't tell me. He knew I'd been a part of the Circle, and he knew I was too emotionally involved." Mr. Solomon glanced, almost involuntarily, at Zach. "I think he was afraid of what I'd do if I found out how close he was getting."

"How close was he?" I asked.

"I don't know." Mr. Solomon shook his head. "But if he was researching Gilly's family"—he pointed to the necklace—"and that makes me think he probably was, then it's possible he was *very, very* close."

Mr. Solomon rubbed his hands on his legs, warming them against the soft flannel. "Patricia," he said, turning to Buckingham, "tell them."

She didn't hesitate or question; she just sat up straighter and said, "What I'm about to tell you may not be true. A lot of people think it's more fairy tale than anything."

"*I* thought it was a fairy tale," Mr. Solomon added. "Almost everyone in the Circle did."

"Yes," Buckingham went on. "You see, to understand, you must first know that before there was the Circle, there was just Ioseph Cavan. But he was a clever man, and he surrounded himself with a trusted band of confidants and co-conspirators. And Gillian Gallagher knew that as long as those friends remained alive and loyal, then the threat Cavan posed could live on."

Professor Buckingham gave a wry smile. "So she went to work. She wanted to identify the members of the Circle—the families that Cavan left behind. The families that rule over the Circle even today."

"So she . . . what? Made a list?" Macey asked.

Mr. Solomon shrugged. "This is where people disagree."

"Yes," Buckingham said. "Everyone knows Gilly eventually married and returned to Ireland, but it is unclear if she continued researching Cavan and his followers. The Circle was far underground then, hiding—even though there wasn't much reason to. The government wasn't concerned about them. Lincoln was dead by someone else's hand, and the country was recovering from a brutal war. The world had enough to worry about. No one was going to listen to the fears of a nineteen-year-old in a hoop skirt."

As Buckingham talked, I couldn't help but remember that there's a reason they call us Gallagher *Girls*. It's not just because the youngest of us are twelve. It's also because our founder was under twenty. From the very beginning we have been discounted and discredited, underestimated and undervalued. And, for the most part, we wouldn't have it any other way.

"No one knows if she finished the list or what she might have done with it." Mr. Solomon shook his head, then smiled. "But I bet your father thought it was real. If he was researching Gilly and her family, then I bet he thought it was real enough to change everything."

"I don't get it," Bex said, sitting up. "What does the Circle today care about a hundred-and-fifty-year-old list of members who've been dead for ages?"

"Because the leadership of today's Circle dates back to that original group," Buckingham told us. "It's essentially a family business. Leadership is passed down from generation to generation. And leadership is a closely guarded secret."

"But if Dad got that list..." I began.

"He would have been able to bring them down," Mr. Solomon finished for me. "He wanted that list because the only way to kill this monster is to learn the monster's names."

"What's the necklace, Joe?" Aunt Abby asked.

"It's the key," I said, thinking about my father's letter telling us he was hiding something precious in that safe on the other side of the world. "Isn't it? It's the key, and my dad was looking for whatever it unlocks, wasn't he? He was looking for that list."

"I don't know," Mr. Solomon admitted. "The stories about Gilly weren't very reliable. Some said she went crazy and that's why she returned to Ireland. Some said she just gave up, moved on, and made babies." He glanced at Macey, the descendant of one of those babies, and added, "Not that I'm complaining."

"Me either," Macey said.

"But Gilly wasn't a fool," Mr. Solomon went on. "If she had something that might be valuable someday, then she was going to keep it someplace safe."

"Locked up with this?" I asked, holding up the necklace one last time.

"I don't know. But if your father hid that away—and he never told me about it—then . . ." Mr. Soloman glanced down at the charm I'd put back around my neck. He didn't say what everyone was thinking—that it might have been worth dying for.

Chapter thirty-five

PROS AND CONS OF BEING ME IN
THE MONTH THAT FOLLOWED:

PRO: Turns out, almost starving to death over the summer means that the school chef will make you crème brûlée any time you want it.

CON: Even crème brûlée gets old after a while.

PRO: Shorter haircuts take way less time to dry and fix in the morning.

CON: The fact that the boy you like *now goes to your school* means you have to fix it every day.

PRO: It's somehow easier to sleep when you finally know where your father is, and that he is at peace.

CON: Not knowing exactly what had happened to him— or to you—means *you* might never be at peace again.

———

When fall ended and winter came, it didn't feel as strange as I'd thought it would. My internal clock had caught up, I guessed. Rain beat against the windows. A chill bled through the stone. And as I sat on the leather couch in a small alcove of the library, a single word pounded in my head: *Gillian*.

That was what the nuns had called me—the name I had said over and over in my fever-filled dreams. Summer Me must have known she was important. Summer Me might have known everything, and suddenly I hated the bump on my head for robbing me not only of my memories but also of my progress.

"Cammie," someone said, but I didn't turn at the sound of the voice.

"Earth to Cammie . . ."

"Cammie!" Macey shouted, and I shook my head and turned to see my roommates standing there.

"Are you okay?" Liz asked.

"I'm fine," I said for 2,467th time that semester. (I know. I was keeping count.)

"I thought you had therapy," Bex said.

"I did but . . . then I came here."

"Okay," Macey said, trying again. "Then what are you *doing* here?"

"Thinking."

Even though the mansion is big and solid and reinforced in about a dozen different ways, I could have sworn I heard the building groan as the wind howled beneath the *peck peck peck* of sleet falling against the walls. It should have been easy to stop thinking about summer. But it wasn't.

"What is it, Cam?" Bex asked, dropping onto the sofa beside me.

"This." I pulled the necklace over my head and stared down at the seal. "It feels like I'm missing something. About it. About Gilly."

"I know," Liz said. "Why have we never seen this before?"

It seemed like a fair question. Our school crest was everywhere, from the brass brackets that held back the heavy velvet curtains to the good china. Gilly had branded every inch of her home with that one symbol as if to make sure we could never forget who and what we were.

"Why haven't *I* ever seen this crest before?" Macey said. I knew where her frustration was coming from. The Gallagher family was her family, after all, but there was nothing I could say to make it better.

"Here," Liz said, sitting upright. She walked to the glass-covered bookshelves and held her palm against the small sensor on the wall. A second later, the protective glass slid aside.

"Are those...?" I asked. Liz nodded and smiled a guilty smile.

"Gilly's original journals? Oh, yeah." Liz shrugged. "Buckingham gave me clearance the day after she told us all about the crest. I've been coming down here in my spare time to read through them."

"Of course you have," Bex said with a grin.

"I always wondered why these weren't in the subs," I said, taking a pair of cotton gloves and a book from Liz. I open the smooth leather cover and looked down at the most beautiful penmanship I had ever seen.

"Well, they aren't really classified material." Liz opened a page at random and started reading aloud. "'Tonight, father sent Elias to see me. They do not want me to include former slaves in my "youthful experiment," as it will make it harder for the school and for me. He simply does not understand what my school is to be—what I am to be.'"

"So Gilly's family . . ." Macey started, but trailed off.

"Disapproved?" Liz guessed. Then she nodded. "Totally."

"Awesome." Macey looked like she'd never been more proud to have Gilly's blood in her veins.

"Yeah," Liz went on. "They wanted her to get married and settle down. In journal seven, Gilly writes about how it was only after her parents died that she inherited the mansion and . . . well . . . the money. That's when she was able to move the school here and expand it. Like Buckingham said, she made a really big deal about putting the school crest everywhere the family crest had been."

"Gilly was awesome," Bex said.

"Yeah," I agreed, turning back to the fire. "She was."

"Does she mention anything about a lock?" Bex asked Liz. "Or the key?"

"You mean the key I didn't even know I had?" I said.

"Cammie, don't be so hard on yourself," Liz said. "We don't

even know that the necklace *is* a key. Maybe it was just some old Gallagher family heirloom your dad found."

Liz could have been right—she usually was. But I didn't feel any better.

I ran my finger across the small medallion. "It feels like maybe I've seen it before, or . . . I'm missing something."

"Well, maybe Summer You did see it somewhere," Liz said, but I just kept looking at the necklace, hearing my father's words over and over in my mind. *Key. Lock. A way for this to be over—a window that can lead to a happy ending.*

"Window . . ."

My voice trailed off as my mind drifted from Dad's letter to the crest I wore around my neck, and then all the way back to the first assignment Joe Solomon had ever given us.

"Bex, do you remember the day we met Macey?" I asked.

"Of course I do."

"Do you remember seeing Mr. Solomon in the corridor? Do you remember what he told us to do?"

"Notice things," Bex said, and with those words, I was gone.

Okay, so I know I've given my best friends a lot of reasons to think I might be crazy, but they seemed a whole new kind of worried when I jumped up from the couch and darted down the hall, through the foyer, and up the sweeping staircase at a full run.

Bex was behind me, Macey following close behind, when I turned on to the wide corridor on the second floor that led to the Gallagher family chapel. It was the oldest part of the mansion and the very place where Bex and I had stood during Macey's first visit to our school. That was where Joe Solomon had told us that covert operatives should not just look—but see.

There was a window overhead, and I heard my teacher's words and stared up at the kaleidoscope of color that I'd walked beneath every school day since the seventh grade—at the stained glass I'd looked at a million times but had never really seen until then. Something about that lesson and that image must have stuck with me all those years. I knew just what I was looking for, exactly where to find it. And when my roommates finally came to stand around me, I raised my hand.

"A *window*," I said, quoting my father's letter and pointing to the stained glass that was different than any other window in the school. There was a field of green, and tall stone walls, which I had always assumed represented our mansion. But that wasn't it. The green field was too open, the blue beyond too vast—like the sea. And in the center of the lines that criss-crossed the window like a labyrinth I saw it—an emblem identical to the one that, for weeks, I had been wearing around my neck.

"There," I said, pointing up at the one image of the Gallagher family crest that remained inside our mansion. "I saw it there."

"It's a picture," Bex said.

I shook my head. "It's a map."

Chapter thirty-six

THINGS TO DO IF YOU'RE GOING TO FLY
ACROSS AN OCEAN TO GO ON A POTENTIAL
WILD-GOOSE CHASE-SLASH-SCAVENGER HUNT:
(A list by Cameron Morgan)

1. Convince your mom, your aunt, and your recently
   comatose teacher that letting you go is a good idea.

2. When number one fails, convince them that leaving
   you behind by yourself is a BAD idea.

3. Pack all your homework to take with you (because
   you really shouldn't waste that time on the plane).

4. Try to relax.

5. Remind yourself that this sort of thing is actually

kind of normal for highly trained government operatives.

6. Pretend like normal is going to be possible for you ever again.

I'd never been to Ireland before. Or at least I couldn't *remember* ever being to Ireland. But as soon as Macey's father's jet began its descent over the tiny airport on the country's western coast, I was certain I was seeing it for the first time. Nothing that beautiful and green could ever be forgotten.

There wasn't even the faintest hint of déjà vu until the jet landed and the door slid open and I heard a deep voice say, "Hello, young lady."

Agent Townsend looked up at us, his eyes hidden behind dark glasses. He seemed especially spylike as he watched my aunt climb out of the plane and come to stand on the tarmac beside him.

"Abigail," he said flatly.

"Townsend," Abby said in reply.

When Mom joined Abby, Townsend gave a solemn nod. "I'm very sorry about your husband, Rachel. He was a great man."

"Thank you," Mom said, and no one dwelled on the rest of it.

"How's Solomon? Mad he's not here, I suppose," Townsend said, walking around the end of the plane.

"Exactly," Abby said.

Dark clouds were brewing in the east, and there was a charge in the air. I could feel the little hairs on the back of my neck standing on end when Townsend turned to me and said, "Well, Ms. Morgan, let's have a look, shall we?"

"Here." I handed him the pictures of the stained glass window.

"And you think this is . . ." Townsend started.

"It's a map," Liz told him.

"See—crest marks the spot," Bex said, as if there couldn't possibly be any doubt.

"You do know about the list Gillian Gallagher was making of the Circle's original members, don't you?" Macey asked.

Townsend laughed a little, as if no one so young and female had ever dared to question him before. She smirked right back, as if he'd better get used to it.

"I know about the *stories*," Townsend said. "And they are just stories, you know? There's never been any proof that Gillian Gallagher started—much less finished—that little quest."

"She did it," Macey said.

"That's very well, Ms. McHenry, but—"

"We think the bank box wasn't empty last summer," Zach said; and that, at last, had Townsend's full attention.

"We think it had *this*." I reached for the thin chain around my neck and pulled the necklace over my head, held it out for my former teacher to see.

No one said anything while Townsend looked between the crest on the necklace and the one in the picture.

It seemed to take him forever to shake his head and say,

"That doesn't mean anything." He took a deep breath and turned to the water, gestured to a fishing boat docked not far away. "But I guess there's only one way to find out."

There is a whole section of our library dedicated to Gillian Gallagher—her family, her life. Her legacy, and her school. I'd read all the books during my seventh grade year, so I knew that Gilly's family had come from Ireland's western coast. I knew that her grandfather was a lord and her father had been a second son. But even though I'd been perfectly capable of finding her ancestral home on a map for years, nothing had prepared me for the boat ride Townsend took us on that afternoon.

The waves of the Atlantic crashed against the rocky shore. My stomach lurched and churned as I stood looking up at the sheer face of the cliff that rose before us, a limestone wall three hundred feet high over the ocean. Water lapped against it, and the boat rocked, enveloped in the mist.

"What's wrong, kiddo?" my mom asked.

"What if it's not up there?" I yelled over the sound of the boat and the roar of the ocean. Mist sprayed into my face. "What if we're wrong?"

Mom smiled. "Then we'll know," she shouted back, and pushed my wet hair out of my eyes. "One way or the other, we'll know."

I saw Zach watching me from the other side of the boat. He smiled. A simple look saying, *It's okay, we have this. Everything is going to be fine.* And more than anything, I wanted him to be right.

By the time Townsend stopped the boat, the sky was an eerie shade of gray, as if the ocean waters and tall cliffs had mixed and formed the clouds that hung overhead, blocking out the sun. The boat rocked, and Liz gripped her stomach. Her face was a pale shade of green.

"Why are we stopping?" she asked, and for a second I thought she might be sick.

"We're here," Townsend said.

"But . . . how are we supposed to . . ." Macey's voice trailed off as she pointed to the top of the sheer cliffs.

Mom and Abby shared a look, but it was Townsend who reached into a chest, pulled out a rope, and tossed it in Bex's direction. "We climb."

I must have been getting stronger.

After the past few weeks, the bursts of mist felt like a shot of adrenaline. The rocks were sure and smooth beneath my hands, carved out by wind and salt water and the power that comes with a few thousand years.

Those cliffs had been there when Gilly was a girl. Those cliffs would be there long after my roommates and I were gone. The thought was somehow comforting as Bex climbed beside me. From the corner of my eye, I could see Zach to my left.

It wasn't a race—I knew that much—but I couldn't help myself from climbing harder, moving faster; sweat and adrenaline were my friends, pumping through my body, reminding me that I was there—hanging off the side of the world. I was alive.

I might not have remembered my summer vacation, but I had lived through it, at least.

My ponytail blew around my face. Mist clung to my eyelashes. There, with the winds that whipped over the Atlantic and crashed against the cliffs, I felt a million miles from the Alps, and I kept climbing.

I could hear Mom and Abby helping Liz, telling her where to put her hands and reminding her that she was safe—they had her. (Not to mention the fact that she'd designed that particular model of safety harness during our sophomore year.)

And then, finally, there was a hand reaching out to me through the haze.

"Hey, Gallagher Girl," Zach said, pulling me onto solid ground. The wind was even harder there, with the ocean stretching out before us, as if Ireland had just sprung from the ocean one day and was still rising. For a second, it almost knocked me off my feet.

"Easy there," Zach said when I stumbled into him. "Now's probably not the time to get handsy. You might want to control yourself."

"I'll try to keep that in mind," I told him, and turned to look around. But there were no power lines or blinking lights; just lush rolling hills that stretched out as far as the eye could see.

And then I saw the castle. Except *castle* wasn't the right word—not anymore. It was more like ruins. Massive stone walls had crumbled and toppled into an honest-to-goodness moat. There were the remnants of barns and grounds, and only the castle's tallest tower was still standing, looking out over the sea. I felt like we'd climbed those cliffs like Jack had scaled the beanstalk, and somehow we'd found our way to another world.

"What happened to it?" Macey asked.

I couldn't tell if she was feeling a pull toward her ancestral home or if she just stepped closer out of curiosity. It didn't matter, I guess. We were all being drawn to those decaying walls and the weed-riddled courtyard like a magnet. It was almost like we were looking at the Gallagher Academy through a funhouse mirror, at what might have happened if the two homes of Gillian Gallagher had shared the same fate.

"Time, Ms. McHenry," Townsend said. "It can be a cruel, cruel thing. The Gallagher family's money ran out about a hundred years ago, not long after your Gilly died, in fact. No one has lived here in decades. These old estates are almost impossible to keep up. Looters and vandals overrun everything. If your list ever was here, Ms. Morgan, it is probably gone by now. Are you prepared for that possibility?"

I swallowed. "I am."

"Okay," Abby said, handing each of us a copy of the window, the map. "We split up. I have a feeling we don't want to be around by the time *that* gets here." She gestured to the storm brewing in the distance.

"Everyone has their comms?" Mom asked, and we nodded.

"Good," Abby said. "I'd recommend we start by trying to locate some of the landmarks on the map and work from there."

She looked at Townsend as if expecting him to protest, but he simply shrugged. "I was about to suggest the same thing."

"Okay, then," Zach said. "I guess it's time."

We started to turn and leave, but Liz yelled, "Wait!" She was pulling off her backpack and reaching for the zipper. "I have some things." Townsend might have rolled his eyes a little, but Liz talked on, handing a plastic bag to every member of the group.

"A flare gun, Liz?" Bex said, staring into her bag. "I seriously doubt we'll need a flare gun."

Liz shrugged. "I believe in being prepared."

"And what's in here?" Abby asked, giving a small vial a shake.

"Aspirin," Liz said. "What? Scavenger hunts give me headaches."

"Are we ready?" Mom asked, pulling us back to the task at hand. Everyone looked at me.

I didn't say what I was thinking: that it might have been nothing. That I may have dragged us halfway around the world and into the center of a storm for something that had never existed at all. Maybe Gilly never made the list. Maybe she didn't hide it there. Maybe it was lost to time or rain or the scavengers that come to pick at the bones whenever any great thing falls.

But we had to look.

No harm could come from looking.

Chapter tHiRty-SeVeN

Number of hallways we walked down: 47

Number of cave-ins and landslides that made us turn around: 23

Number of times Bex pretended not to be terrified of a spider: 14

Number of places where the four stories had pretty much fallen together like a stack of pancakes: 9 (that we came across)

Number of times Liz almost fell into the moat: 2 (not counting the time Bex threatened to push her in if she didn't stop messing with her flare gun)

I went through an archaeology phase when I was ten. I spent that whole summer digging behind the barn on my grandparents' ranch, unearthing arrowheads and old screws, trying to fill in the pieces of a story I didn't even know.

That was what being there felt like.

There were walls and rocks, weeds and moss growing over crumbling staircases and ancient pillars. The whole thing was layered with dust, and we walked for hours, climbing over fallen stones and decaying beams. But as we spread out and climbed, I had to wonder if it was more wild-goose chase than mission. After all, the map wasn't really a map. It was more of a kaleidoscope of images spread across a green field. There were trees and cliffs, a book and a cross. And the crest—the image from the necklace—sat in the center of it all. It might have made sense once upon a time, but over a century and a half later, I stood with my best friends and Zach, staring at the old stone walls and barren gardens, wondering if we were looking at a lost cause.

We found broken pieces of furniture and old iron fixtures, but nothing that seemed to belong in this century or the last. It felt like we were walking back in time, and with every step, my hopes fell until finally we made our way into the center of the ruins.

The walls were still standing in that part of the castle, and for the first time, something seemed oddly familiar. I looked at my best friends and watched their eyes scan the ancient space.

"Is that a fireplace?" Bex said, pointing to a pile of crumbling stones.

"Look at the way the walls curve," Macey said, her gaze panning around the strangely shaped room. "It's almost like . . ."

"The library," Liz said, and immediately I knew that she was right. It was exactly like the library at the Gallagher Academy, from the position of the fireplace to the tall windows that overlooked the grounds.

"How do you know?" Zach asked.

Liz looked totally insulted. "Because . . . uh . . . library."

"Okay." Zach threw up his hands. "Point taken."

"The book," Bex said, pulling out a picture of the window and pointing to the image of an old book, which filled one part of the stained glass.

"Of course!" Liz said. "So if book equals library, and we're standing *in* the library, then the crest should be"—she turned like a human compass, trying to find north—"that way."

The good news was that Liz was right about the direction. The bad news was that her finger was pointing at a massive pile of debris. Sure, there had probably been a hallway there, once upon a time, but by then the walls were nothing but fallen stone. Our way was undeniably blocked.

Thunder rumbled in the distance. The light that filtered through the glassless windows was eerie and the color of the sea.

"I don't like the sound of that," I said.

"Neither do I," Bex agreed.

"Maybe we should split up and find a way around," Zach said. "Cam and I will take the right. You guys go left. If we're lucky, we'll meet here." He pointed to the place on the window where the crest hopefully marked the spot.

"Fine," Bex said, but she didn't sound happy about it. "See you there," she told me.

"See you there," I agreed. And a moment later they were gone, and Zach's hand was in mine, pulling me into the black.

I'm not sure what it says about us, but it felt almost like a normal date—two kids exploring ruins, digging in the dirt. We climbed over fallen beams and crawled beneath crumbling archways. As sad as it sounds, it was almost romantic.

After a while I said, "We're getting close." It wasn't that I knew it—it was that I felt it. There was something calling to me, pulling me through the dark passage. Zach was at my back, trying to keep up.

"Cammie, wait," he said. "Cammie—"

"It's blocked." I stared at the stones that had fallen, filling the narrow doorway. Only a small hole remained near the top. "I think I can . . ." I said, starting to climb; but Zach grabbed my waist and set me back on the ground.

"No," he told me. "I can't fit."

"But I can." I began to climb again.

"Stop." Zach reached for my arm. "It's too tight."

"No. I can make it."

"Gallagher Girl, we can find a way around."

"It's in there, Zach. I know it's in there. Let me go get it." My voice cracked. "Let me go get what my father wanted me to find."

He didn't want to let me go—I could see it in his eyes. But there was no arguing with me. Not then. I was going with or without him. There was no asking for permission. So he squeezed my hands and kissed me gently. "For luck," he

258

said, then stepped aside to let me climb the rocks and squeeze through to the other side.

"What do you see?" he yelled, once I was out of sight. I sent my flashlight across the stone walls and dirty floor.

"Not much," I said, and began to climb down the other side. But as I moved, the shifting of my weight caused the stones to move, cascading into a cloud of dust until Zach and the small ray of light behind me disappeared completely.

"Cammie!" I could hear him. The word was sheer panic. "Cammie, are you—"

"I'm okay!" I yelled back through the stone. "I'm fine, but we're never going to be able to move all this rock." I shined my light around the room. Twenty feet away, I saw what I was pretty sure had been an exterior wall, but decades of decay had done their damage, and now there was a small hole, dim rays of sunlight shining through.

"There's a hole in the outside wall. It's not big, but I think I can get out that way," I yelled. "Just go around to the outside and meet me there."

He must have heard me, because there were no protests from the other side of the stones, and I was left alone with my thoughts and my flashlight and the music that was in my head, growing louder.

I let the flashlight play across the walls and the floor until the light came to rest on a small stone outcropping that looked something like an altar. Dust and dirt covered the stone, so I used my hands to brush the years away, and that was when I felt it—a small indentation no larger than a quarter.

I ran my finger along the edges and stared down at the Gallagher family crest, exactly where the window had said it would be.

"I found it, Daddy."

Part of me said I should wait for someone—to do something to mark the occasion. But I didn't have the time or patience to delay. I felt my hand trembling as I went to the chain that hung around my neck and pulled the necklace free.

"Could it be this simple?" I asked myself, looking down at the small emblem.

I couldn't breathe, couldn't blink. I didn't say another word while I pressed the small pendant against the hole in the ancient slot and twisted. The whole world stopped as the stone slid away, revealing a narrow compartment full of cobwebs and shadow and a small tube sealed with wax, which felt like the most precious thing I'd ever seen.

My hands shook. My heart pounded. But I knew exactly what I was doing as I pulled the tube from the compartment and held it gingerly in my hands. . . .

And heard the words, "Now, I'll be taking that."

Chapter thirty-eight

She was there. The woman from the roof in Boston and the tombs of Blackthorne. The woman who was Zach's mother.

Zach's mother was there.

She stepped from behind a pile of debris and stood silhouetted in the fading light that sliced through the narrow gap in the wall. I wanted to be wrong, but there was no mistaking her voice or her form and, most of all, the sick feeling in my gut that came from the sight of her.

She was there, standing between me and my only means of escape.

"How did you find this place?" I had to know.

"Oh, I could ask the same of you. *I've* been coming here for years." She walked through the ruins as if she had pulled the castle down stone by stone until she finally found me and that moment.

"Then why didn't you just take it?" I asked, bile in my throat. "You take everything else."

"Oh, I would have," Zach's mother said.

She's Zach's mother.

She's Zach's mother.

She's Zach's mother.

"But Gilly . . . she was as pesky as all Gallagher Girls seem to be."

I looked at the box I'd just opened and saw the intricate mechanism that lay inside: gears like clockwork surrounding a small compartment filled with gunpowder I didn't dare to touch.

"Nineteenth-century explosives?" I asked.

"Oh, yes," Zach's mom said.

"So Gilly booby-trapped it?"

I remembered Townsend's distaste at the word and felt a nervous laugh rise up in my throat. It was all I could do to swallow it and not let the terror take hold.

"You're going to give me that list, Cammie."

"No." I shook my head. "I'm not."

She held out one hand as if I were going to just hand over the very thing my father had died trying to find. "Cammie," she said, impatience ringing through her voice. *"Now."* The comms unit in my ear was as dead as it had been in Rome. I was alone when she said, "Come now, Cammie. We got to be so close last summer. . . ."

The lie was cold and empty, and yet the smile was a real one. She was happy to be there, taunting me.

"It is so good to see you strong and well." She talked on, then glanced down at the cylinder in my hands. "Now, hand me that very carefully."

But I just held the thing that Gilly had hidden away—held it like my very life was trapped inside, and I didn't dare let it out of my grasp.

When I didn't move, Zach's mother cocked her head. "Cammie," she said, and slowly began to hum, "do you hear the music?"

I *did* hear it, and I wanted to say so, to tell her that it was always there in the back of my mind, pulsing and beating like my own heart. It was even stronger then. I felt myself start to sway, a quiet rage building, and yet I did not move to fight, to scream. It was as if I were frozen there, waiting . . . teetering . . . and then . . .

Dust filled the air. Bits of rock scraped my face and arms, and the force of a blow knocked me to my knees. When the smoke began to settle, I could see that the small hole had become a massive, gaping opening. The exterior wall was practically gone. There was absolutely nothing standing between me and Liz, who shrugged. "I also packed explosives."

There was no time to hug her, because I was already pushing through the rubble, grabbing her hand in mine, and yelling, "Run!"

It had started to rain. Cold drizzle turned to pounding, piercing drops as we ran, sliding down a steep embankment, the ruins at our back.

Liz's bag fell off her shoulder and tumbled across the rocks, leaving a trail of books and markers and tranquilizer darts. There were a scary number of tranquilizer darts. She stopped as if on instinct to reach for her things, but I pulled on her arm.

"Leave them!" I cried just as I felt a blow to my back. I fell, crashing against an outcropping of rocks, and slid across the wet stones that ran like giant steps lower and lower, closer to the cliff's edge.

My right arm slammed against the ground. Pain shot from my elbow to my shoulder as if lightning had struck; and I couldn't help myself—my hand fell open and the cylinder flew from my fingers and skidded across the massive slab of stone, falling to the ledge below.

"I told you to hand me the list, Cammie."

I rolled over and looked up. Zach's mom was standing behind me. The wind was so much stronger there, blowing against her wet hair. Rain ran down her face and clung to the corners of her mouth.

"It's not like you even need it." She laughed. "You're the one person on earth who doesn't need it. Now, give it to me!"

What did she mean I didn't need it? I didn't know—didn't care.

"You want it," I told her, climbing to my feet. "Come through me and get it."

"Cammie, no!" Liz cried, just as a gust of wind blew from the sea and almost knocked me off balance. I glanced to the ridge below and saw the cylinder beginning to roll, closer and closer to the edge until . . .

"No!" I yelled, lunging for it, sliding across the wet ground. But it was too late. The precious thing was falling end over end through the rain and the wind, crashing to the stormy sea below.

From the corner of my eye, I could see a helicopter sitting on the hillside, its blades starting to spin. There was a distant crack of gunfire, muffled by the sounds of the storm. And there, on my hands and knees, I looked for any thing—any way—to make Zach's mother hurt as much as I hurt.

Rain pounded against my face, and I crawled—the wet stone hard on my knees, grappling until I felt the barrel and the trigger, and stumbled to my feet.

The flare gun was in my hand, and my hand was pointing at her chest. I could feel my body moving independently from my mind again. The haze and the fog filled my head. I was aware faintly that my friends were there yelling, "Cammie! Cammie!"

But the list was gone, drowned in the ocean, broken on the rocks and dissolved in the rain. My father had looked for it. My father had died for it, and it was gone. I would never see either of them ever again.

So I raised the gun higher and fired.

Red streaked across the sky. With the flash, I looked down at my arms and remembered the way the red drops had stained the ground, the way the cold water of the river had felt so good against the gashes and scrapes.

I remembered water and running.

I remembered how to survive.

"Oh, Cammie, you are such a good girl," the woman said, and I honestly couldn't tell if it was supposed to be an insult or a compliment. There wasn't time to ask, because she was already stepping toward the cliff, saying, "I'm sorry it has to be this way."

And then Zach's mother raised up her arms and jumped, diving into the waters below.

My first thought was that I had to get the vial. To find it. If it had survived, then . . .

I had to follow.

"No!"

I felt arms grasp my waist and draw me back.

"Let me go, Zach."

"No, Cammie!" It was Bex's voice, clear and strong.

"No, Gallagher Girl," Zach said, holding me tighter, whispering in my ear. "It's gone."

Chapter THiRtY-nine

I know the flight home wasn't the longest plane ride of my life, but it felt like it. The ocean was so vast outside my window, and all I could think was that the list was out there somewhere. Sitting on the ocean floor. Smashed against a rock. Or maybe floating like a message in a bottle, bound to someday turn up on a distant shore.

But I didn't know. And I probably never would.

When we finally reached the mansion, Zach insisted on walking me to my room.

"Excuse me, but aren't boys forbidden on this floor?" Macey said on our way to the suite.

"That's the advantage of being the only boy," he said. "No one actually comes right out and makes rules like that."

It sounded like a fair enough point, and Macey shrugged. We were all too exhausted to argue.

The halls were dark and empty. The only light came from the emergency exit signs, and the whole school seemed to be sleeping around us. My classmates didn't know how close we'd come to finishing my father's final mission. If I had my way, they never would.

"What's wrong?" Zach said, stopping me and reading my mind.

I shrugged. "What isn't?"

My elbow throbbed. My head ached. And I was pretty sure I was having the worst hair day ever, but when he grabbed my hand and pulled me to him, I didn't protest.

"Hey," he said. "It's going to be okay. You'll get some sleep. And everything will look better in the morning."

Sometimes the best advice is the simplest—every good spy knows that. So I chose to believe him.

He kissed me on the forehead and started back the way we'd come, but at the last second I called, "What's her name, Zach?" He turned back to me. "Your mother . . . I don't even know her name."

"Catherine. Her name is Catherine." Then he smiled a little sadly and went downstairs.

Even after I woke and got out of bed, I didn't feel better. To tell you the truth, I didn't feel anything. I was faintly aware of the fact that the halls were empty, the corridors quiet, as I walked alone to the closed door and raised my hand to knock.

"Come in! Come in," a voice yelled, and the door creaked open. "It's good to see you, Cammie." Dr. Steve put a book into a large satchel, then snapped the lock and gestured to the chair beside the fire. "I appreciate your coming so late."

"It's not late," I said, then glanced at the window and saw that it was dark outside. I looked down at my legs and remembered I was wearing my pajamas.

Dr. Steve walked around his desk, took the seat opposite mine. "I heard about what happened in Ireland, Cammie. And I wanted to know . . . how are you?"

It was a question I'd heard a lot in my life. *How's your head? How's your safety? How's your heart?* So I answered as truthfully as I could.

"I don't know."

"I can imagine that you might feel sad and confused after what happened. It's only natural. Here"—he handed me a piece of paper—"I find that it can be very helpful to write those feelings down."

"I'm sad and confused," I said, writing out the words. "It's only natural."

"Of course it is." He leaned forward, looked at me through the light of the fire. "Do you get tired of wearing that necklace, Cammie?"

My hand went to my throat. "This necklace?"

"I feel foolish for not realizing what it was earlier. But of course you didn't have it at the stone house."

"No," I said. "When I was in Rome, I mailed it to myself with a bunch of other jewelry."

Dr. Steve laughed. "You're a very smart girl, Cammie."

"Thank you."

"That's why you're such a formidable opponent for the people who have been after you."

"I guess," I had to admit, but truthfully I didn't feel formidable in any way.

"Tell me about that song, Cammie."

"What song?" I asked.

"The song you were just singing."

"I wasn't singing any song."

"Yes you were. It was this song."

Then Dr. Steve pushed a button and I heard it—I really heard it—the music that had been playing inside of me from the moment I woke on that narrow cot.

I felt myself begin to sway, and when Dr. Steve said, "Sing it, Cammie," I began to hum because there were no words.

"Do you remember the first time you heard that song, Cammie?" Dr. Steve said softly.

"It was the week before my father disappeared—the day he took me to the circus."

"That's right. Think about the circus. It's like you're there now. What do you see?"

"There is a lion tamer and some clowns and—"

"Where is your father, Cammie?"

"He's beside me. We are walking through the crowd. A woman is stopping in front of us. She's dropped her purse and he's helping her. There's a napkin on the ground."

"What does he do with the napkin, Cammie?"

"He offers it to her, and she says, 'No, that's trash.' Then he puts it in his pocket and leads me away." My voice was flat, but something in my mind recognized the scene for what it was. "It's a dead drop."

"It is," Dr. Steve said.

"There's a list of names written on the napkin. It's the list that Gillian Gallagher wrote. I am supposed to remember that list."

I knew it was true—that it was right—but even as I spoke the words, there was something in my mind, like a tiny ripple on a perfectly still pond.

"Dr. Steve," I said, my voice slightly stronger, "how did you know it was a stone house where they held me?"

Dr. Steve smiled. "Because I was there, of course."

"Of course," I repeated, and I honestly felt embarrassed that I hadn't remembered. It was like I'd failed a test, and I wasn't looking forward to the day when Mr. Solomon found out. "I'm sorry I forgot."

"Don't be. We would never have let you escape if we weren't certain we could *make you* forget."

"So I didn't block it out because it was too painful? I didn't . . . mess up?"

"Oh, no, my dear. You did exactly as we needed you to do. And it almost worked. We got so much further here—in the safety of your school—than we did on the mountain, didn't we?"

"Yes," I said.

"We learned so much. But, of course, we never quite learned what we were looking for. A part of you always resisted. . . . You never quite let us in."

"I'm sorry," I said again.

"Oh, that's okay. We were worried for a while, but now that

we have the original list that Gillian hid in Ireland, it doesn't matter."

"But I saw the vial go over the cliff," I said, thinking about Zach's mother and her long dive to the rocky waters below.

"Yes. But it didn't break, and dear Catherine was able to retrieve it. So now we have it, you see." He smiled at me kindly. "Which means now, I'm afraid, we don't need you."

I actually felt ashamed. I didn't like being unnecessary—a disappointment. There had to be something else I could do, so I asked, "But . . . why? If you're part of the Circle, why would you need to know what Gillian learned about the founders of the Circle?"

He chuckled his *aren't you adorable* laugh. "Now, Cammie, you know that I'm just a lowly worker bee. No one knows who the heads of the Circle are. No one knows who calls the shots—the *inner circle*." He smiled at his own cleverness. "Do you think the CIA and MI6 are the only ones who would like that information?"

"So the Circle has a splinter group?" I asked.

He nodded, eyes wide in the dark. "Yes. There are people within the Circle who want very much to use that list. And there are other people—powerful people—who would gladly kill you to keep it from ever being found."

I watched him shiver as he sat by the fire. All the color drained from his face. "I was so afraid they were going to kill you, Cammie." He nodded slowly. "And they would have, eventually. The people in charge would have sent more snipers, other grab teams. They wouldn't have stopped until you were—"

"But now they will stop?" I asked, hopeful.

"Yes. Now it all will stop." He nodded and patted my hand. "For you."

"I just want it to be over," I said.

"I know, Cammie. Write that down," he told me, so I did.

It felt so easy, sitting there by the fire. So peaceful. I'd never known how much work it was to think, to worry, to feel.

"You're very tired, aren't you, Cammie?"

"Yes," I said.

"That's okay," he told me, and pointed again to the paper. As I wrote how tired I was, he talked on. "We've been working so hard to help you remember what you saw at the circus. But now you don't have to remember anymore. In fact, now I need to make sure no one ever questions you again. Would you like that?"

"Yes," I said. It sounded like the sweetest possible release.

"Trust is an important thing to an operative, isn't it, Cammie? Important to a girl." Dr. Steve moved a little closer, looked into my eyes. "Do you trust me?"

"Yes," I said.

"Good. Now, I need you to go to the terrace beside Madame Dabney's tearoom. You're going to stand on the balcony and watch me drive away. When I'm safely out of the gates, I need you to jump."

"When you're safely out of the gates, I'll jump." I stood to leave, but something stopped me at the door. "Dr. Steve," I said, thinking of the gun in my hands in CoveOps, the shot I didn't remember firing on the hill. "Did you teach me how to kill?"

"No." He shook his head slowly. "You mastered those skills all on your own." He picked up the bag that sat beside his desk and reached for his jacket. "It's been very nice knowing you, Cammie. Good-bye."

"Good-bye, Dr. Steve," I said, then climbed the stairs and went to the fifth floor to die.

Chapter forTy

I didn't pass a soul on my way to the fifth floor. It was almost three a.m., the perfect time for roaming the halls unobserved. Too late for the night owls finishing papers and cramming for tests. Not yet time for the early birds who liked to start the day with a solid workout in the barn or by checking on an experiment in the labs.

So I was alone, walking through the dark halls that I know better than anyplace else on earth.

I didn't try to hide the sound of my footsteps. I wasn't careful with the doors. I wasn't breaking any rules, wasn't hiding or sneaking. I was just a girl following the orders of a teacher as I reached the fifth-floor landing and opened a window to step onto the small balcony outside.

The only thing I regretted was that I hadn't gone to get a coat. Oh well, I thought, putting my arms around myself, inching closer to the edge. I wouldn't be cold for long.

I couldn't see the main gates from where I stood, so I

climbed over the railing and dropped onto the sloping roof, inching around the corner of the building until the freezing north wind blew into my face.

The past few days had been filled with sleet and rain, and the whole roof was covered with ice, so I had to be careful where I stepped. Dr. Steve had told me to wait until he was through the gates, and I didn't want to fall too soon. A lot was riding on my getting it just right.

I reached up and touched the necklace at the base of my throat. I had only worn it for a few weeks, and yet it felt like part of me. It was the last thing my father would ever give me—his final gift. Tears filled my eyes, and I shook my head, trying to toss the thought aside, but that just made me lose my balance, skid a little, so I stopped and stood perfectly still, my eyes on the gates.

The music was louder then, and I hummed along with it, remembering that day in the sixth grade when Dad came home with two tickets for the circus.

I was too old for the circus, I'd told him.

"That's funny," he'd said. "I'm not."

And so we'd driven all the way across Virginia. Four hours in the car, just the two of us, talking and laughing and eating peanut M&M's until our fingers looked like rainbows.

I was going to be going away to school soon, I'd told myself. He wanted to do this while he could.

Standing on the roof, I remembered the way my dad had watched the people on the high wire. It had looked so easy. But it couldn't really be that easy, could it? So I stepped along the narrow tiles of the roof, my arms out wide.

276

Yes. It *was* easy.

"Cammie, sweetheart," someone said, "I want you to walk over here."

I turned and saw my mother behind me, easing from a window and out onto the icy roof.

"Mom!" I yelled, happy to see her. I pointed my toes and moved my hands. "It's like the circus!" I cried, and in my head, the music was louder.

"Cam." Bex was climbing over the balcony railing, easing toward me from the other direction. "It's okay, Cam. We're here. Let's get you inside now."

"My dad took me to the circus, Bex. Did I ever tell you that?"

"Sure, Cam," she said.

I glanced at my mom. "You weren't there," I told her. "I think you were in Malaysia."

"Let's go inside and talk about it, kiddo."

"Bex, have you ever wanted to be on a high wire?"

"No, Cam, I want to go inside."

"Don't you love that song?" I asked, and began to sing.

"Come inside, Cammie," my mother said.

"Cammie!" Liz's cry pierced the air. It was part scream, part screech, and I thought she must be hurt. She was at the window above me, and before I knew it, she was climbing through.

"Lizzie, stay there!" Bex cried, but Liz didn't listen. "Liz, watch out for the—"

And before Bex could finish, Liz's right foot landed on a piece of ice and she lost her hold on the windowsill. She was sliding, falling faster and faster until she finally caught hold of a pipe that stuck out of the roof. Her small hands gripped it, holding on for dear life.

"Liz!" Bex yelled, and moved toward her; but the ice was too thick. She started to skid, and stopped, frozen, unable to move.

"Cammie . . ." The worry in my mother's voice had turned to panic. "Cammie, come over here to me."

I heard her say it, but my gaze was locked on the gates, the taillights disappearing beyond them.

"It's time," I said.

"Time for what?" my mother asked.

"Time for me to jump," I said, certain of what I had to do.

I looked out across the frosty grounds of the school, so peaceful and serene while the rest of my sisterhood slept. I raised my arms and—

"Cammie, don't!" Liz screamed, and moved too quickly. The pipe she was clinging to broke free from the roof, and then she was falling, sliding.

I was supposed to jump. It was time. I'd been given a direct order, and I was the kind of Gallagher Girl who always follows orders. Wasn't I?

But there was Liz, sliding down the steep pitch of the icy roof, and I fell to my stomach, stretched out, and caught her small wrist so tightly that I feared it might break, but I held on anyway.

We were at the edge. Liz's small body was swaying back and forth like a pendulum in midair. Tears streaked down her face.

And still, part of me couldn't help but notice how Dr. Steve had passed through the gates by then. There were other things I was supposed to do.

"Liz, I'm going to swing you up onto the roof, okay?"

"No!" Liz screamed. Her voice was a broken, terrified sob. "No, Cam. No. No."

"It won't hurt, Liz. I'll swing you just like—"

"Cammie, no!" Mom yelled, but it was too late. I was already moving Liz's thin frame, swinging her back and forth.

"Bex, get her!" I yelled and threw Liz in Bex's direction.

It seemed to take forever for her to fly from my hand and onto the patch of icy roof at Bex's feet. But she was there.

She was safe.

And the taillights were still fading, growing smaller and smaller in the distance. I knew the time had come.

I was almost too late.

The music grew louder, but rougher too—like a record that has been played too many times.

The taillights disappeared.

I knew I was *supposed* to go, but I looked back at my friends and my mother one final time, turning too fast on the ice. I felt my feet slip as the high wire became too much for me, and I was gone. Sliding. There was nothing beneath me but cold wind. Nothing above me but sky.

But the fall didn't come. I looked up to see my mother gripping my left arm, my best friend holding my right. Behind Bex, Liz was scampering through the window, yelling for help.

I should have weighed too much for them to hold on to

for that long, but neither hand that gripped mine even shook. They would have held me forever while I dangled there, legs floating free in the breeze while Dr. Steve's taillights faded into the night.

"We have you, Cammie," Bex said. "We have you."

My mom didn't say anything. Tears dripped off her face and onto mine as I stared up at the woman I wanted more than anything to become.

"Do you hear the music, Mom?"

"No, sweetheart. No. I don't hear it." She shook her head. Terror and tears filled her eyes.

The wind felt colder, washing over me.

"Neither do I."

Chapter Forty-One

"**M**om," I said, over the din of people yelling and running. There were orders and lights—so many lights. "Mom, Dr. Steve...he had me. Last summer he had me and then he wiped my mind and came here and..."

"I know, kiddo. I know. Now rest." She looked up and screamed down the hall, "Patricia, where are the doctors?"

"Mom, it was the circus."

"It's okay, Cammie. You're safe." Mr. Solomon was there, leaning by my mother's side.

"No, Mr. Solomon. You don't understand." I felt a sharp prick in my arm, and my eyes got heavy. The words slurred, but I talked on. "Dad took me to the circus, Mr. Solomon." My head began to sway. "He took me to the circus. And then he died."

And then I slept.

When the sun broke through the windows of my mother's office, it felt like the brightest light I'd ever seen. I blinked and turned, the leather couch soft and warm against my face and hands. Zach leaned against the wall, staring at me.

"You know," I whispered, "some girls might think it's creepy having a boy watch them sleep."

He smirked and pointed to himself. "Spy."

"Oh." I nodded. "Right. So you're a *trained* Peeping Tom."

"Product of the best peeping academies in the country."

"Well, now I feel much better."

"You should."

He was beside me then, his arms wrapped around me, holding me tightly.

"I'm not crazy," I whispered.

"I know."

Believe it or not, that's the most romantic thing Zachary Goode ever told me.

And I kind of loved him for it.

I heard the door open, and in a flash, the room changed in a flood of people.

"Cammie!" Liz yelled. "Oh, Cammie, I was so worried when you . . ."

But she couldn't finish. I was glad of it. I'd never been so humiliated in my life. Weak. I felt weak. And the mere thought of what I'd let myself become made me want to hurl myself off the tallest tower again (this time for an entirely different reason).

"Oh, Cammie. Oh, Cammie," Liz went on, breathless and gasping for air. "You're okay. You are okay, aren't you? You don't have any more headaches or—"

"I'm fine, Liz," I said, but the expressions on my three best friends' faces reminded me that they'd all heard that before.

"I *think* I'm fine," I said, with special emphasis on the word. "I feel different."

Macey eyed me. "You look different." She touched my hair. "Seriously . . . *conditioner.*"

"It's good to see you too, Mace." And it was.

Mom and Abby sat on the coffee table in front of me. Bex and Macey stood hovering at their sides. Mr. Solomon was leaning against my mother's desk. It was far too reminiscent of the morning after the election the year before, when I'd woken with the knowledge that the Circle was chasing me—that they wouldn't rest until they'd found me.

Sitting there that morning, it might have been easy to think that nothing had changed, but that was wrong. Everything was different.

I was different.

"It was the circus," I told them. In the cool light of morning, the words must have sounded more sane than they had the night before, because no one rushed to calm me this time. Everyone waited.

"The CoveOps report," Liz said. She pulled a chair closer and sank onto it, as if my words had knocked her off her feet. She reached for her bag and found the dirty copy I'd retrieved from the embassy in Rome.

"What does that have to do with . . ." Bex started, but Liz was already turning to the page where I had talked about going to the circus with my father. It was nothing, really, a sentence or two that could have just as easily been left out.

And if I had left it out, then my life probably would have turned out very, very differently.

"I saw something that day," I told them. "Dad met with an asset. And the asset gave him a copy of Gilly's list—the one he was trying to find. The one in Ireland." I shook my head. "He must have gotten the key somehow—hidden it in Rome and gone looking for the map. But he never found it. He never *had to* find it because someone gave the whole list to him right before he disappeared."

"Who?"

I tried to remember, but the woman was a blur, her face nothing but shadows. "I don't know. But the Circle wants that list . . . or . . . *part* of the Circle wants it. They've wanted that list all along."

I told them everything then—about the splinter group and how traitors can happen on both sides of the law. And, last, I talked about how they'd had me and interrogated me and then wiped my mind and let me escape just so they could keep on interrogating me in the place where I felt safest.

It takes a lot to make people who know fourteen different languages speechless, but that did it.

When Zach said, "I'm going to kill Dr. Steve," it wasn't the angered threat of a worried boy; it was the calm, cool statement of an operative trained to do exactly that. And that, I think, is why it scared me.

But it wasn't as terrifying as the look in Bex's eyes when she said, "Not if I find him first."

I couldn't say I blamed them. After all, I know a lot of guys like to play games with a girl's head, but Dr. Steve had taken it to a whole new level.

It seemed to take forever for Mr. Solomon to move to the window and say, "So they're staging a coup."

"Figures," Zach said with a shrug. "If I know my mom, that's about her style."

"I don't understand," Macey said, shaking her head. "I don't understand why Zach's mom needed you alive—"

Bex finished. "And her bosses want you dead."

"Because I've seen the list."

In my mind I heard the circus music, made myself hum the song, and, with it, the memory came rushing back. I saw my father and read the words on the crumpled napkin. And then I knew what they had wanted—what part of the best criminal organization in the world had chased me to find.

What the remainder would kill me to hide.

"Your mom was right," I said to Zach, somehow amused. "I didn't need the copy Gilly hid in Ireland. I had it all along."

Outside, sleet was falling, and in the warmth of my mother's office, the windows had started to fog. I was faintly aware that I was standing. The window was cool beneath my forefinger as I ran it through the dampness on the glass.

"Cam, what are you—" Bex started, but Liz said, "Shhh."

And I started writing.

It was like the gun in CoveOps, like the way the assassin's rifle found its way into my grasp on the hill. My hands were not my own, but that time I knew they were moving, and I didn't want them to stop.

When I ran out of space on the first pane, I moved to another. And then another. I could feel my roommates and Zach lurking, reading the words that I left. Drops of water bled down the glass, running line into line, but I couldn't stop.

I had to keep writing until . . .

"Cam, is that . . ." Liz started.

"Elias Crane," she said, looking up at Mr. Solomon, who nodded.

"The head of the largest agrichemical corporation in the world has that name. I'd wager it runs in the family."

"Charles Dubois," Liz offered another.

"There's a Charlene Dubois with the European Union," Abby said, running her hand through her hair. "Half the defense spending on that continent goes through her."

There were four names that no one recognized immediately, but I kept writing until—

"Mrs. Morgan?" Liz's voice was timid, afraid. "Do all the Circle heirs go . . . into . . . the business?"

"It's unlikely that leadership would come from outside sources," Mr. Solomon said. "They're very secretive, girls. More so even than the CIA."

"But . . ." Liz went on, eyes wide. "Does it ever . . . skip . . . a generation or something?"

"Why?" Bex asked.

Liz took a deep breath, then she pulled me away from the window so that the others could see. "Because the last name on the list is Samuel P. Winters."

Chapter forty-two

PROS AND CONS OF THE WEEK
THAT FOLLOWED:
(A list by Cameron Morgan)

PRO: Knowing finally that you really were crazy for a little while. But it's over now.

CON: Craziness (temporary or not) is usually followed by very strange looks from underclassmen.

PRO: Once you finally remember something—like a song that's been bugging you—you can stop singing it. Forever.

CON: There's nothing like being brainwashed and manipulated for several months to make a girl wonder if she'll ever stop doubting her own judgment.

PRO: Discovering a clue that could help eliminate a major terror organization means some of the coolest spies in the world spend time behind your mother's office door (especially spies named Mr. and Mrs. Baxter).

CON: Try as you might, that door stays closed to you.

———

I've grown up in the halls of the Gallagher Academy—I know the floors that slant and the stairs that squeak. I can walk them blindfolded (a fact scientifically verified by Liz during a particularly long snowstorm during February of our eighth grade year). But after that . . . after that they felt different—like I was seeing them for the first time in months. Like a window you don't know is dirty until it's been cleaned. In the week that followed, I saw everything with a new light.

I saw everything.

Ambassador Winters hadn't saved me in Rome. He'd cornered me. I played it back, over and over—the alley he'd tried to get me to go down, the fake police officer he'd wanted me to trust. He'd been so close to ending me—ending this. But he hadn't.

A week after Dr. Steve left, I was lying with my best friends and Zach on the mats of the P&E barn, staring up through the skylights at the moon. We should have been studying. We should have been worrying about final tests and projects and papers. But our books lay unopened around us. The questions on our minds hadn't come from any class.

"Hey, Cam," Liz said, breaking the silence. "There's something I don't get."

"What's that?"

She propped herself up on an elbow. "Preston's dad. Why did he show up at the bank? Why didn't he just let them kill you?"

It was an excellent question—one I'd thought about off and on for days. "I think . . ." I started slowly. "I think he wanted to find out what I knew—what I remembered about the list. About last summer. I think he didn't want to kill me if he didn't have to."

But he *did* have to, and, thankfully, no one said it.

"You okay?" Zach asked. He looked like he was about to pick me up and run back to the doctors as fast as he possibly could.

"Yeah," I said, then squeezed his hand and smiled. "I am." If I sounded surprised, I guess . . . I was.

I stood and walked to the heavy punching bag, hit it once and watched it swing back and forth, its shadow swaying across the floor. It reminded me of the way Liz had dangled, freezing and terrified, off the roof.

"When did you know?" I asked, turning to them. "You did know, didn't you? That something about me wasn't . . . right?"

A guilty look passed over Liz's face, but Bex didn't bat an eye. "We always knew."

"But—"

Bex shook her head, dismayed. "You were losing time, Cammie. When have you ever lost track of time?"

She was right. I should have known something was wrong, but I guess, as a spy, sometimes the biggest lies we tell are to ourselves.

Through the windows of the barn I could plainly see the lights burning in my mother's office, but I knew the door was still closed to us. Locked. Try as we might, the five of us were not going to be invited inside anytime soon.

"They're working late tonight," Bex said. She followed my gaze and probably read my mind.

"Did your mom and dad say anything to you before they left?" Liz asked Bex, who shook her head.

"Just that we don't need to know," she huffed, and I knew the feeling. It's a phrase that all spy kids eventually grow to hate.

"It's not fair," Liz said. "They wouldn't know anything if it weren't for Cammie. And us. I can't take this." She was up and pacing across the mats. "I. Can't. Take. This. This is torture." Then she looked at me. Her eyes got big. "Not that—"

"It's okay, Liz," I said. "It's a turn of phrase. You're forgiven." I forced a smile, but my mind lingered on the word.

Torture. I'd been tortured. And for the first time that semester, I allowed myself to realize that my mother was right. There are some things you really don't want to remember.

"Okay, I got it," Bex said. "Tonight, after everyone goes to bed, we break into your mother's office. And we bug the place. Now, I know it won't be easy, but—"

"No."

My friends turned to me.

"But we've done it before," Liz countered.

"I'm not saying, *No, we can't do it.* I'm saying, *No, we shouldn't.*"

"But . . . why?" Liz asked.

"Because if we were supposed to know what is happening in that room, we would have been invited into that room," I said, and smiled at Zach. He'd been right, of course, and I looked down at the mat. "Because there are things you just can't un-hear. No matter how much you want to."

I didn't know what was happening in my mother's office. But I had a hunch. There were so many leaks, moles, and double agents within the CIA and MI6 that whatever happened next had to be orchestrated very carefully. And, besides, Gilly had hidden that list away a hundred and fifty years ago because people weren't going to take it—or her—seriously.

Some things never change.

"What's taking so long?" Liz asked. "I mean . . . Cam told them who the leaders of the Circle are—or who their relatives were. That's the hard part. Can't the CIA and MI6 and every-one just . . . round them up?"

"It's not that easy, Liz," I said.

"But—" Liz started.

"But we aren't the only ones looking for them." Zach walked to the window. "She's out there. And she wants them even worse than we do."

He was right, of course. Catherine was out there. Dr. Steve was out there. The weight of it bore down on us all until—

"We've got to get Preston." Macey's voice was flat and even. It was the first thing I'd heard her say in hours, I realized. She'd been sitting, thinking, planning that whole time, and when she spoke, it wasn't the erratic, emotional response of a girl with a crush. It was the well-reasoned argument of a Gallagher Girl with a plan.

"Zach's mom and the splinter group are going to be coming

for Preston's dad—maybe for Preston too. We have to get him out of there."

"I don't know, Macey," Liz said softly. "We can't just fly to Rome and . . . take him."

Macey pointed to herself, but there wasn't an ounce of tease or humor in her voice when she said, "Jet."

"But . . ." Bex started. "You're talking about kidnapping an ambassador's son."

"No. I'm talking about *saving* him," she countered. "Either you're with me or you aren't, but I'm not going to sit here and let him get sucked into whatever his freak-of-nature birthright is supposed to be. I'm not going to stand by and let him be collateral damage. Or worse."

"Macey . . ." I started, and she wheeled on me.

"He helped you, Cammie. You had no place to go, and he helped you."

"I know, but—"

"But what?" she snapped. "Preston isn't like his dad. He's the family disappointment." She sighed. "Trust me. I know it when I see it."

And I believed her. Maybe because I liked him. Maybe because I'd had enough of traitors for one semester. But more than that, it was because Macey was a Gallagher Girl, not just by training but by blood. She wasn't going to get that one wrong.

"Macey, Preston's dad is an ambassador," Zach said softly. "The embassy is a fort. If I know my mom, she'll go after the softer targets first. And we don't even know that they will go after Preston."

"But they might. They might and—"

"Okay," I said.

"Okay what?" Bex asked.

"After finals and winter break . . . after I'm back to full strength, we'll go get Preston. Whether Mom and Abby and Joe and Townsend like it or not, we'll go get him. And then . . ." I trailed off. "And then we'll finish this. Next semester, this thing ends."

Walking back to the room that night, I tried not to think about all the things I still didn't know. Like where Dr. Steve had gone, or how to find him. Or who the asset was that my dad had met at the circus and how she'd gotten a copy of Gilly's list. I didn't let myself fixate on exactly where and how Summer Me had messed up and let herself get captured.

Those questions would come back eventually, I was sure. But not then. Then, there were other questions on my mind. Like what was going to be on our Countries of the World final and exactly how much fudge Grandma Morgan was going to make me eat over winter break as soon as she saw how skinny I was.

The seventh graders ran by, one semester older. Just like us. And it hit me: they hadn't gotten smaller. I'd just gotten bigger. Stronger.

And then I let myself realize the one fact I'd been too afraid to admit: no one is chasing me anymore.

Now, even as I write this, Gilly's list is still in my mind, crystal clear and waiting. For me to be rested. For us to be ready. For a new semester and a new chance to finish the work that Gilly and my father started so many years before.

Now I know that, from this point on, we'll be the ones doing the chasing.

And I like it.

Acknowledgments

There are so many wonderful things that have come with writing the Gallagher Girls, not the least of which is the sisterhood that has grown up around the series. I'm so grateful to Catherine Onder, Stephanie Lurie, Deborah Bass, Dina Sherman, and the rest of the Disney-Hyperion family who have given the Gallagher Girls such an amazing home and stood by them through the good times and the bad. Kristin Nelson and everyone at the Nelson Literary Agency continue to prove why they are the best in the business and are so instrumental in everything I do. I owe so much to Heidi Leinbach, Jen Barnes, Holly Black, Rose Brock, Carrie Ryan, and Bob, who are always there to help and support me in so many ways. And, of course, I am indebted to my family, especially my father, mother, and big sister. Last but certainly not least, I thank the readers everywhere who have gone on these adventures with Cammie and proven that real Gallagher Girls do exist, even if the school is fictional.